LP W HAMMER Chad
Hammer, Chad.

D0381089

SPECIAL MESSAGE TO READERS

This book is published under the auspices of

THE ULVERSCROFT FOUNDATION

(registered charity No. 264873 UK)

Established in 1972 to provide funds for research, diagnosis and treatment of eye diseases. Examples of contributions made are: —

A Children's Assessment Unit at Moorfield's Hospital, London.

•

Twin operating theatres at the Western Ophthalmic Hospital, London.

•

A Chair of Ophthalmology at the Royal Australian College of Ophthalmologists.

•

The Ulverscroft Children's Eye Unit at the Great Ormond Street Hospital For Sick Children, London.

You can help further the work of the Foundation by making a donation or leaving a legacy. Every contribution, no matter how small, is received with gratitude. Please write for details to:

THE ULVERSCROFT FOUNDATION,
The Green, Bradgate Road, Anstey,
Leicester LE7 7FU, England.
Telephone: (0116) 236 4325

In Australia write to:
THE ULVERSCROFT FOUNDATION,
c/o The Royal Australian and New Zealand
College of Ophthalmologists,
94-98 Chalmers Street, Surry Hills,
N.S.W. 2010, Australia

COME SEE ME HANG

The law said wild Johnny Toro must hang and the Governor ordered he would die in his squalid hometown — to teach respect for the law. Gunfighter Clay Stocker seemed an odd choice to send down to keep the peace until young Johnny swung. A lot of men could go down before he mounted the gallows. But Stocker would survive. He always did. He was that kind of man.

Books by Chad Hammer
in the Linford Western Library:

HARD COUNTY GUNDOWN
BLOOD JUSTICE
THE CHOSEN GUN
JUST CALL ME CLINT

CHAD HAMMER

COME SEE ME HANG

Complete and Unabridged

LINFORD
Leicester

First published in Great Britain in 2007 by
Robert Hale Limited
London

First Linford Edition
published 2008
by arrangement with
Robert Hale Limited
London

The moral right of the author has been asserted

Copyright © 2007 by Chad Hammer
All rights reserved

British Library CIP Data

Hammer, Chad
　　Come see me hang.—Large print ed.—
Linford western library
1. Western stories
2. Large type books
I. Title
823.9′2 [F]

ISBN 978–1–84782–394–6

Published by
F. A. Thorpe (Publishing)
Anstey, Leicestershire

Set by Words & Graphics Ltd.
Anstey, Leicestershire
Printed and bound in Great Britain by
T. J. International Ltd., Padstow, Cornwall

This book is printed on acid-free paper

1

The Gunfighter

He was limping long before he reached the bridge. That made two of them footsore, Stocker and his big ugly horse both.

It was three hours since the sorrel had thrown a shoe. Stocker calculated he'd walked ten miles in total darkness since then but it felt more like twenty now.

It was enough to be lamed and exhausted in the dark of a Southwestern Territory night, but that wasn't all.

The moment he reached the old bridge he felt it. Something wasn't right. Either the borderland midnight was too quiet, or maybe his horse's ears were pricked too high. The man grunted dismissively, deciding he was simply too damned weary to tell good from bad, danger from normal.

He halted and the horse shook its head, bridle bit chiming softly.

The sagging town sign he'd glimpsed nailed to a tree back a ways had read 'Mesa Vista'. His lip curled. A better name might be Scum City from all he'd heard.

He shrugged and spat. He wasn't here to like or dislike, he reminded himself. Just to see the job done right.

Hang Toro.

Then go.

Keep it simple, hero!

From force of habit he loosened the heavy gun in its holster before moving on. Legs aching, loose boot sole flapping, shoulders sagging. Someone had dubbed him 'Last of the Straight-backs' in his early days in the trade, but they wouldn't have thought so tonight. He'd been dubbed with other names far less flattering.

He was moving slowly now but his eye was as sharp at midnight as it had been at high noon.

That was how a man stayed alive in his business, and Stocker had survived longer than most.

The horse stumbled again and the man grunted 'Oats.' Shaking its big head in response the sorrel picked up its gait as they came off the old bridge and trod the worn track leading into Mesa Vista.

Stocker halted abruptly.

The town was now dimly visible directly ahead. He saw where his poorly lighted street led into the plaza with a glimpse of a skinny church with a high bell-tower. His eyes were gritty from days of heat and dust yet he was alert as always and missed no detail along that pueblo-lined street.

So, why had he propped that way? the back of his mind wanted to know. *Looks normal, doesn't it?*

He had to concede it did. At first. But then again came the sensation that all was not quite right. He couldn't name what it might be but knew he would not move another inch until he had identified what it was.

Seconds stalked the eyelocked silence, and then came the sound. It was just a rustle in the deepening quiet but it caused his neck hair to lift and saw his hand go to gun handle.

After a long moment he went on again, but now his .45 filled his hand. Then came the roar of the hidden gun and the gout of orange flame blossoming like some rare desert flower flared from the alley-mouth and sent a slug whistling over his head.

The crash of the shot blended with the responding thunder of his Peacemaker as he homed it in on the phantom shape dimly visible beyond the low wall.

A man coughed and cried out in agony. Stocker triggered twice more, his trajectory lower each time as he followed the falling shape to the ground.

Still in a crouch, Stocker waited with every sense alert, searching for further danger. The horse had shifted some distance off but now stood waiting as it was trained to do, looking back at him.

'*Dios mio . . . Dios mio . . .* '

The agonized words were followed by a cough, then silence.

Expelling a held breath, Stocker covered the distance to the alley with a swiftness that had surprised many an enemy before.

Before reaching the crumpled figure he methodically dumped the spent shells and reloaded. He transferred the piece to his left hand before reaching down to shake the man's shoulder.

'Why'd you try to kill me?' he demanded.

The man groaned. In the half-light it was plain to see he was Mexican, small and shabbily dressed with the stink of a long-unwashed body rising up. A gun lay beside him. Stocker picked it up with a sneer. It was an ancient single-action Avery conversion model .44 with rust showing around the chamber.

He shoved the piece in his belt. 'All right, scum — why?'

The man rolled his head towards him, eyes bugging. He made an attempt to reply but the cough came again, shaking his emaciated frame. Finally he managed one tortured word.

'Water . . . '

'The hell with that. You'll talk first, you lousy son of a — '

'You . . . ' Again the look of hatred. Then, with an effort terrible to see: 'You . . . you are the governor's butcher gunman . . . sent here to see Toro will dance upon the air!' An agonized intake of ragged breath. 'But I would kill you first . . . K-kill the evil gunman . . . '

Stocker rose to his full height to stare about him at the alien nightscape of tumbledown adobes and broken fences, beyond them sickly paloverdes silhouetted dark and motionless against the faint glow of the lights.

Nothing else. No heads bobbing from windows, no curious figures spilling into the streets. Certainly no sign of a sheriff although he knew they had one here.

The man moaned for water again. Stocker stared at him without emotion. Then he turned and, with sixgun still in hand and every sense alert, returned to the horse and unstrapped his canteen.

He toted it back to the Mexican. 'Here,' he grunted, dropping to one knee and unscrewing the cap. 'Here's your lousy water . . .'

He stopped and peered closer. The man was staring straight upwards and was no longer coughing. Stocker put an ear to the bloody chest then straightened and replaced the cap with an expression of disgust.

'So much for a secret mission!'

He spat in the dust.

'That's all your word's worth, Ballentine!'

In that moment he despised both the governor of Southwest Territory and his ramshackle administration, yet still knew he would not quit. Could not.

He would stay on and see Toro hang.

* * *

Stocker snapped his fingers and the sorrel limped across to his side. He hefted the corpse and slung it across the horse's hindquarters where it hung limply like a bundle of old rags. He looked down disgustedly at the blood-spatters on his own shirt and swabbed at them with his bandanna, then headed on towards the lights.

Still no sign of life upon the square, the only sounds those of hoofs clopping in the quiet, and his broken boot-sole flapping again.

He paused upon reaching the plaza. It was a big square for a town its size, wide and treeless. Six street-lamps cast a feeble orange glow over adobe and brick.

He now had a full view of the Spanish church directly opposite. Alongside the church stood a house of the same early design with a small wooden cross upon the roof . . . the padre's quarters.

On either side of the church buildings were weed-choked yards contained by low adobe walls supporting wrought-iron gates flaked with rust.

The remaining frontages of the town square were fully built out by cantinas, liveries, stores, a solitary hotel and the flat-roofed jailhouse. One whole side was occupied entirely by three big haciendas, white-washed and with iron-barred gates, plainly the residences of the town's wealthy citizens.

His lip curled as his gaze swept the remaining three sides.

What a pest-hole!

He trudged on, feeling again the same intangible atmosphere of decay and brooding menace that had first struck him on the outskirts. Pest-hole, for sure, but maybe more dangerous than it had appeared at first glance.

He paused again to focus on the structure which arose ominously in the square's centre, adding the final dark touch to the scene.

Built upon the cut stone base of some ancient construction, with high wooden steps leading up to it on one side, the gallows stood tall and gaunt against the sky.

Stocker's expression showed no change as he trudged on by. He'd seen too many such structures in his time, with too many men kicking their lives away at the end of rope, many of them guilty.

He eventually drew up before the squat stone building with the words SHERIFF'S OFFICE burnt with a branding-iron into a slab of pine nailed above the scarred old door. Chinks of light showed behind drawn shades and while he looped the horse's lines around the hitch rail he thought he heard the scuffle of movement within. Yet when he mounted the porch and rapped hard upon the oaken door, there was no reply.

'Sheriff!' he shouted, echoes booming across this too-empty square. No response. He hit the door harder with an impatient fist. 'Hey, inside, get this damned door!'

Silence. Stocker fingered eye-sockets with a weary gesture. Long miles, broiling heat, lamed horse and a five-hour walk topped off by a gunfight.

10

Might as well admit it, he was one beat *hombre*. And staring at a bloodied corpse draped across his horse didn't boost his spirits one lick.

He crashed his boot into the base of the door.

'Sheriff Tite Fulton! You in there?'

This time he heard the scuffling again, followed by the faintest of whispers. He kicked the door again, angry now, timbers threatening to give way under his onslaught. The door opened a crack and a rifle barrel poked through the gap. In back of the weapon he caught an impression of a pale face and fearful eyes.

'Who're you?' the man asked nervously. 'What do you want?'

'Are you Fulton?' Stocker demanded.

'No . . . jest a minute . . . '

The rifle was withdrawn, the door closed again. That did it for Stocker. Backing up two paces, he then slammed shoulder into the door with all his strength. Screws popped and a metal hinge struck something glassy with a crash. Hanging by a single hinge the door collapsed inwards and Stocker found himself facing a frightened deputy clutching a rifle with an older man staring over his shoulder.

'Hey!' The haggard man wearing a sheriff's star panted with obvious relief. 'You ain't one of Toro's hellions!'

'I gave my name,' Stocker snapped. 'Anyway, what sort of an office are you running when a man has to kick the door down to get your attention? What happens if somebody needs the law in a big hurry?'

But he'd already lost their attention. Both peace officers were now staring out at the horse with its grisly burden. They seemed frozen by the spectacle, while the newcomer shouldering his way into the centre of the office didn't help ease their shock any.

'He tried to dry-gulch when I crossed over the bridge,' he growled. He paused upon noticing the naked revolver in the older man's fist. Stocker grabbed gun handle and backed up a pace. 'Unhook yourself from that hogleg and do it fast, mister! I won't say it twice!'

The man shook visibly as he shoved the .45 into leather. Stocker stared at him closely, puzzled.

'You Sheriff Tite Fulton?'

'Y-yes I am. And you'd be . . . ?'

Stocker realized the man had been drinking. The whole place stank of liquor. He regarded drinking as a weakness. He hated weaknesses.

'Stocker, I said. OK, we've got that straightened out, so now hear this. I just arrived minding my own business when this geezer cut loose on me from in back of the bakery. I shot him, and now you, as the lawman of this dump, you are going to take custody of him and write up a report. Anything there you can't get your head around?'

Shocked but sobering fast, the lawman studied Stocker a moment longer before going to his doorway and peering out again.

He appeared even shakier as he turned back to the room.

'That's Lobato,' he muttered. 'No-good bum with four starving kids. Why in hell would he want to shoot up a stranger? Did he say anything before he croaked?'

'Not a word,' Stocker lied.

The lawman dropped into a battered desk chair and brushed a hand over his face. After a moment he started in talking as if to himself.

'Nothing but trouble and strife ever since we locked that killer up here . . . I warned them it would only start more trouble than this town had ever seen . . . and the Lord knows it's seen plenty . . . '

'Are you talking about this Toro character now?' Stocker guessed.

'That's the party. The meanest heller in the territory he was . . . then the border patrol catches him and dumps him in my cells and says they aim to hang him here!'

He paused, blinking owlishly. 'You see them gallows on your way in?' Stocker nodded and Fulton went on:

'Hang Johnny Toro? I said. Why, every border hellion from here to Hellfire looks on him like some kinda god, not the mother-killing scum he is. And so the government takes it into its head to hang him down here where they figure it will do the most good. *The most good?* Good for who?'

Stocker knew all this and more but said nothing for the moment.

As though exhausted by his outburst, the lawman resumed his moody staring, muttering under his breath.

Stocker's face was taut with contempt as he swung upon the deputy. 'Go get that carcass off my horse.'

'What'll I do with him?'

'Whatever you like!'

The man hurried out and Stocker swung back on the sheriff. 'All right, tell me where I can get a room and a stall for my horse.'

'What do you want a room for?' Fulton asked stupidly.

'To sleep.'

'Sleep! You want to sleep? Everybody

15

wants to sleep in Mesa Vista — but scarce anybody does any more!'

The lawman appeared almost hysterical as he jumped up and began waving his arms.

'I want to sleep. Kwell here would just love a good night's rest. And our goddamn mayor is falling asleep at midday because he can't sleep nights. And the reason he can't is on account of him and everyone else in town is convinced that before we get Toro up on the gallows his gang's going to try and bust loose and maybe kill all of us in our beds for our trouble — '

'Look, damnit — ' Stocker tried to cut in, but the sheriff would not be silenced.

'Everybody in Mesa Vista wishes they could sleep, Stocker. But the only man who sleeps good night after night — just like you can wager he's doing right now — is *him*!'

He jerked his thumb towards the archway leading back into the cells, shivered. '*Sleeps!*'

Stocker's contempt showed plain as he stared down at the man. He span on his heel and went out through the broken door. The body was gone, no sign of the deputy. Nor of anybody else. A man had been killed, a lawman had shouted a drunken tirade — yet the broad plaza remained as empty as a whore's dream. What the hell sort of town was this anyway?

He must remember to thank the governor for talking him into this one.

He led the horse out of the square and down one of the narrow streets that ran off the plaza like the spokes of a wheel.

He came to a courtyard and entered by a narrow laneway. The open space was lined with heavy shading trees and a busted fountain occupied the centre. He was groggy from exhaustion but his right hand didn't come off gunbutt until he'd led the sorrel into the stables. He stripped him down, watered him and closed the door before heading back across the courtyard with his warbag slung across one shoulder, his right boot-sole flapping still.

He'd seen some rough days in his time but this one had to rate close to top of the list.

Donna Salla's two-storeyed rooming-house backed on to the cantina yard.

A small nightlamp illuminated the patio of the rooming-house. A note weighted down by the lamp informed what rooms were vacant upstairs, with the message repeated in Spanish. He selected a key marked 3 and went up the wide adobe steps on the outside wall of the building.

He let himself into his room, struck a vesta and lighted a candle on a bench against the wall. The room was small, with a bureau, washstand and bunk. The one window overlooked the lane he'd followed in. A Navajo rug covered the floor and the walls gleamed with fresh white-clay paint.

He grunted in satisfaction. The place was clean, very clean, something he had not expected to find in Mesa Vista.

The low bunk looked enticing and he was aching in every muscle as he unpacked his gear. He stripped to the waist and treated himself to a thorough sluicing down with cold water and lye soap, the light sheening upon his lean-muscled torso as he scrubbed.

He wiped his face and studied his reflection in the framed mirror above the washstand.

No change, he mused. *I still look the same . . .*

Ever since he'd killed his first man . . . so long ago now it seemed . . . he'd always had the impulse afterwards to see if the death had left any mark. He reasoned a gunman's face should betray some hint of his trade.

But again, broad forehead, lean cheeks and hard jawline appeared about the same as always apart from the lines of exhaustion which would likely be gone by the time he awakened.

What had that hot-bodied woman in Wichita told him once? 'You look like a man who has seen everything, Clay Stocker.'

Yeah — everything.

He tossed the towel aside and turned away.

Cleaning the Peacemaker was a nightly ritual that never varied. He then hung the gunrig on the bedstead by his pillow where it would be within easy reach. After checking the lock on the door he kicked off dusty boots and blew out the candle.

He lay in the hushed darkness with a pallid slice of moon casting the window square upon the far wall as he waited for sleep.

So far, no good, he mused cynically.

The governor had conned him, some shambling bum had tried to murder him, the sheriff whom he might have to rely upon was a jittery boozehound, his horse was lamed and it seemed likely most everyone suspected who he was and the reason he had come.

He smiled mirthlessly in the dark. At least the governor had displayed a glimmer of honesty when hinting he might not find his job of keeping the lid on Mesa Vista until the hangman arrived to swing the killer, to be without risk.

His eyelids fell. One man dead and the job not properly begun . . . how many more to die? One thing was for sure: Stocker would ride away from here at the end of it no matter how many others didn't.

Deep, even breathing filled the room and he was asleep.

2

The Governor

'Name?'

'Gallardo, señor.'

The short man with the broadcloth jacket and oiled hair was stationed before the governor's oaken door. The ragged peasant stood before him, hat in hand, while beyond him, lining the forty-foot long corridor, stood another dozen men and women.

'Half the goddamn county,' the short man snorted to himself. Then, 'Well, what in hell is your problem?' he demanded irritably.

The man looked nervous. 'Please, I wish to see the governor.'

'What for?'

'It is the governor I want to see,' the man insisted shrilly. 'He always say he see anybody who is in trouble. I got trouble . . . so he see me. No?'

'The governor is a busy man. You must tell me why you want to see him first.'

The peasant looked sulkily down at the hat in his hands and said nothing. The official glared at him and swore. Then he swung on his heel and rapped sharply on the door behind.

A voice sounded through the door. He opened it and leaned his head in.

'What now, Briggs?' The voice was deep and authoritative.

'Another whining wetback, Governor. Won't tell me what he wants.'

'Show him in.'

The man opened the door fully and the ragged peasant shuffled in to stand in awe before the greyheaded man who glanced up from a great pile of papers before him. Briggs closed the door behind him and came round the side of the desk.

He said, 'Name's Gallardo, sir. I calculate he's one of them coming up from the south looking for work in the orchards.'

'Sit down, Gallardo,' the governor murmured. He waited until the supplicant had lowered his ragged ass into a fine leather chair. 'I'll be with you in a moment.'

He returned to his papers and for a time the scratching of his pen was the only sound to be heard. The Territory's new governor was a thin and rangy man with chiselled features and honest eyes. His hair was long and neatly brushed and bushy sideburns were a concession to vanity.

After some minutes he set his pen in a holder and leaned back in his chair, hands linked across his weskit as he studied his supplicant.

'Very well, what is your trouble, Señor Gallardo?'

The man leaned forward, his eyes suddenly bright.

'Is it true what they say?' he said. 'That you are going to hang the Toro?'

Ballentine stiffened, blue eyes sharpening like a spark coming off rock. The man Briggs reddened and snapped,

'You told me you had troubles, mister. What in hell's the idea of you pushing in here and taking up the governor's precious time with something that's none of your business, you lousy little scut?'

He would have said more but Ballentine silenced him with a gesture as he came to his feet. Nervous, the peasant also jumped up, dark eyes wide.

Ballentine spoke soberly. 'Mr Briggs is right, Gallardo. I have many things to do if I am to succeed here . . . important things. Johnny Toro has been tried and found guilty of murder and we also know him to be guilty of many other dastardly crimes. The death sentence has been passed and it will be carried out on the appointed date. Your obvious loyalty and concern, and that of many others like you, is badly misplaced. I ask you then to be on your way and go search for a job. You can help us become strong and independent — not go wasting your time and energies on a man like Toro.'

The peasant's eyes didn't stray from

Ballentine during the lecture. The courage he'd screwed up in order to be able to take this daring step was fast diminishing in the face of this stern countenance and commanding voice. But he cleared his throat nervously and found the nerve to continue.

'Toro is much man,' he said softly. 'In the south he is loved by the people. There will be grief if he is hung.'

The governor sighed patiently.

He had heard the same infantile spiel many times during the past week. Personally he would like to have the supplicant booted clear out of the building in order that he might get to return to his work on real problems. But he reminded himself his task was to debunk the Toro legend as much as to eliminate the man himself.

He said gravely, 'Toro is simply a murderous little outlaw, Gallardo. Have you ever met the fellow?' The man shook his head and Ballentine continued: 'I thought not. You people have managed to make some sort of hero of him, not because he has ever done anything for your welfare but simply because he has always flouted authority and thumbed his nose at the law. It is only because you resent that law and chafe beneath it that you find a man like this admirable. Well, I have pledged myself to enforce our new regime of law and fair play for all. I have also vowed to eradicate the Toros. And that I shall do.'

The peasant was silent. His awe of this impressive man and his big, high-walled room with its draped flag and walls of books was overwhelming. He wished he were back in the cantina lifting a glass and boasting of his 'great *compañero*', Johnny Toro — whom he had rarely ever seen and never met.

The governor stretched out a hand. The peasant gaped, then took it hestitantly.

'Goodbye, Gallardo.' Ballentine smiled. 'Mr Briggs, will you kindly show our visitor out.'

Briggs ushered his man through the door. He spoke briefly to an aide in the corridor, then returned to the big room, shutting the door behind him.

'Drink, sir?' he queried.

Ballentine was standing at his window, hands locked behind him, staring down into the square.

'No thank you, Briggs.'

'I thought you might need one after that, sir.'

'What I need, Mr Briggs, is receipt of the news that Johnny Toro has been hanged. That will do me more good than all the brandy in this territory.'

'It's still more than a week until the date of execution, sir.'

'I know, I know . . . ' Ballentine stared out through the window again. 'Eight days, to be exact. Not long under some circumstances, an eternity under others. Can Stocker keep the lid on that town until Toro is dead? It's a great deal to ask of one man; too much, perhaps?'

'It is still my opinion that we should have dispatched a company of cavalry down to that pesthole, sir. That would have ensured security and placed it beyond all doubt that that murdering bastard would swing.'

'You know as well as I do I didn't have the personnel for that, Mr Briggs. We have crime-waves erupting faster than we can keep up and I need every single man we've got, both up here and available. Besides, I don't want to establish the reckless precedent of deploying soldiers on every pretext. I demand that towns like Mesa Vista develop a respect for the letter of the law and the ability to enforce it. Stocker is there simply to ensure that they respond to that law and learn to like it.'

'Yes sir.'

Ballentine selected a cigar from a silver box on the desk. Briggs was quick with a match. The governor drew deeply then gusted smoke at the ceiling.

'You don't have to remind me that Toro is far from being just another outlaw, of course. I know it. Just as I know that that apology for a sheriff they have in that benighted town would be better suited to digging ditches in Mexico. Unfortunately, it's impossible to rid oneself of all the deadwood at once.'

'I'm sure of that, sir. But what I don't understand really, is — why Stocker? You despise his kind. I've heard you remark a hundred times that gunfighters as a breed should be exterminated and all reference to them erased from the records. You call them legal murderers. And yet you hand Stocker an assignment, and a highly paid one at that.'

Again the steely look came to the governor's eye.

'I gave it plenty of thought, Briggs. I knew I needed a special man. Not one connected with the law, as that might defeat my purpose. I needed a man of ability who might go there incognito and move amongst the people, get to understand them. Such a man who would smell trouble first then knock it on the head before it might erupt. I am sure Stocker will do the job well.'

Briggs shrugged resignedly. He was still far from convinced the governor had made the right choice, but he knew that when his superior had made up his mind there was no shifting him.

He went to the door. 'Who will you see now, sir?'

'Who's waiting?'

'There's a Texan seeking a permit to take trade goods into the strip, and a bunch of Indians who complain that someone is poisoning their wells.'

Ballentine sighed. There were always more. No matter how long or late he worked, there were always more waiting to see him. More and bigger complaints. He glanced at a sheaf of papers on his desk. Health permits mainly. He'd been avoiding dealing with them for a week, they'd have to be attended to now.

'I'll take care of these before I see anybody else, Briggs.'

'Yes, sir.'

The man went out and closed the

door, leaving the governor staring blankly at his windows.

It was the tension over Johnny Toro that was interfering with his work, he realized, rising to pace the office floor. Hiring Stocker and bundling him off to that benighted county had seemed a way out of his difficulties, yet Briggs had stirred a few doubts. Sure, the gunfighter was capable; he'd proved that often enough. But was the breed reliable? Surely it was unnatural for an intelligent man to settle for the life of a hired gun? Who would wish to do it? And he supposed he could be wrong about Stocker's seemingly high character and intelligence?

From his windows Ballentine could see the new Territory flag hanging limply in the still heat. He knew he could not afford a failure in Mesa Vista right now. Should Toro evade the noose it would be like a signal to the entire lawless south-east sector of the Territory that his government was no more to be respected than those weak, corrupt administrations which had preceded it.

He sighed windily. 'In that case, Stocker must succeed,' he muttered grimly. 'He simply must.'

★ ★ ★

The desperadoes stared at the floodwaters in bitter-lipped silence, the moon half-hidden by scurrying border clouds,

At last the leader turned his head, spat into the river and massaged the back of his neck.

'So,' he said with bitter resignation, 'we shall just have to wait until it subsides . . . and so must Toro.'

'We dare make Johnny wait?' another said, shocked.

The leader made a gesture. 'He will understand,' he said, more with hope than certainty. Then, after a moment, 'But just remember, there are others besides us who would give their lives to save Johnny's. If we fail to get to Mesa Vista in time, they will not.'

'You hope!' a runty killer said.

'I know!' retorted the leader. And wished to hell he felt as sure as he sounded, otherwise it might soon be all over for Johnny Toro.

3

The Prisoner

Stocker stood on the shadowed porch of Armijo's cantina overlooking the square.

It was the hour before noon and the town was busy with everyday activities, women browsing at store windows and buckboards creaking to and fro. Nearby, a fat little man industriously washed the windows of his tortilla shop.

Today Mesa Vista lacked some of the sinister atmosphere of the previous night. By daylight it more closely resembled the type of place so familiar along the border, a piece of old-time Mexican life with sun-soaked adobe, deep shade and an air of unruffled calm. There was a genuine air of laziness and quiet, but with a note of music underlying it, perhaps a hidden streak of red in this sun-soaked mosaic that spoke of indolent men who yet could fight, of dark-eyed women waiting for nights and lovers.

It was also a town that could produce a Toro, he mused. Don't forget that, gunfighter.

He glimpsed Deputy Kwell emerge from the law office and make his way along the rickety walk. Stocker turned his head as the man approached. Kwell spotted him and immediately appeared uncomfortable. Tipping his hat jerkily, he made to hurry on by.

'Kwell,' Stocker growled, returning his gaze to the plaza.

The lawman stopped uncertainly. He fidgeted some, then moved warily across to the edge of the porch where Stocker leaned against a stanchion, thumb hooked lazily into gunbelt.

'Yeah, Mr Stocker?'

Still facing away, Stocker said, 'You take care of that feller I shot?'

'Yeah, saw to it first thing. They boxed him up neat right off. I seen the padre too. He'll say the words over him.' The deputy shuffled his feet. 'Er, he . . . the padre that is, he asked me how he come to get drilled.'

'What'd you tell him?'

'Well, just what you told us, I guess. He didn't say nothing, just shook his head and looked kinda sad.'

Stocker watched a low wagon laden with wet cowhides rumble by, axles screeching for a greasing. The deputy lingered uncertainly, unsure whether the gunman had finished with him.

Stocker said, 'Tell the sheriff I'll stop by later to take a look at Toro.'

'Yeah, I'll tell him.' The man hesitated, then said, 'Well, I better be moseyin' — '

'I ain't finished yet,' Stocker mumured. He drew an envelope from his hip-pocket, took a letter from it and studied it. 'Where does Don Luis Trinidad live?'

'Don Luis? Why, that big white house standing by itself on the far side of the plaza.' The man indicated a spacious dwelling with a long, low pillared veranda. 'Don Luis is about the most respected man in town — the whole county, I figure. Everyman and his dog sits up and takes notice whenever he goes by. Er, you a friend of his'n, Mr Stocker?'

'No.' Stocker studied the impressive building a moment. 'He live alone?'

'Nope, got a daughter. Maria is her name and she is one hell of a good-looking woman, too. Not like some of the crows a man sees around these dusty old streets . . . '

For the first time, Stocker turned to face the deputy squarely.

'See you around, Kwell.'

The man reddened. 'Huh? I mean, oh yeah . . . sure, around, right.'

Plainly relieved to be dismissed Kwell fingered his hatbrim and in his eagerness to be on his way fast almost cannoned into a fat lady on the veranda bench, upsetting her basket of apples. She cursed the man as she bent to retrieve the fruit, showing scant respect for the law. Apologizing and tipping his hat again, the deputy scurried away.

Stocker stared bleakly after the man, shaking his head, then stepped down from the veranda. Small wonder Ballentine felt he was obliged to send someone like himself down here to stiffen the law's sinews some.

He made his way to the mail office located between the harness shop and feed store. Inside he took out a letter and studied the address before handing it to a clerk. It was addressed to Governor Ballentine and contained his interim report on his movements and progress thus far, including cryptic comments concerning the leaking of his mission.

He also added his account of his gunsmoke welcome and its outcome. 'That should improve his liver ... I don't think,' he murmured as he quit the building.

For a full hour the newcomer with the thonged-down Colt .45 wandered the streets and alleyways of Mesa Vista.

He soon realized that all the substantial buildings in the town were located on the square. The dozen narrow streets and alleyways leading off it were jammed with squat adobe mud huts, fetid little holes with dusty yards and no windows. Slatternly women and grimy urchins bobbed in and out of these miserable dwellings like so many rabbits.

Few Americans were to be seen abroad at this time of day. He figured the town must look pretty much the same today as it had hundred years back. The mud and squalor had a permanent look.

After circling the town he paused by the tired brown stream a short distance below the bridge he'd crossed upon his arrival.

Now it was alive with women and children involved in the noisy business of washing clothes, then beating them clean with flat boards upon the rocks. Most of the women were dirty and care-worn, but scattered among them were several girls who were yet to succumb to the ravages of hard work, hopelessness and the tedium of their environment.

He raised a boot on to a log and focused on one girl in particular, a half-Mexican with honey-colored complexion and a tumble of raven hair hanging down her back.

She was a real looker, he decided. She wore the thinnest of cotton dresses, the lush full lines of her body showing through clearly. He watched her for a while before realizing that she was returning his look.

She smiled flashingly and called, '*Buenos dias!*'

He nodded, surprised by her friendliness. During the morning he had been greeted by scowls, sneers, the odd muttered oath, the obscene gesture behind his back. Plainly everyone knew by this that he was the government man who had gunned down one of their fellow citizens overnight. He figured it might be too much to expect they'd understand he'd been dry-gulched and had simply reacted the way any man might.

Not that this mattered a damn, he

told himself. He was here to enforce the law, not win friends.

After he'd lingered a spell with a stogie, the handsome girl straightened her back, dumped her washing into a wooden tub and walked up the banks towards him. Expressionless, he studied her, the sensuous grace of her stride, her gently rolling flaring hips.

She halted before him, hands on hips.

'I am Carla Salla,' she announced, as though this was significant. When he frowned faintly, she added, 'You are staying at my mother's house.'

'I didn't know Donna Salla had a daughter,' he murmured. 'How did you know me?'

She gestured eloquently with both hands.

'Strangers are few in Mesa Vista, señor. My mother told me a handsome Americano had come in during the night, and when I saw you I knew you were the one.' She cocked her head to one side, appraising him boldly again. 'I would not say you are handsome, however. But do not be offended. For I must say you do carry yourself like a conquistador . . . and your eyes are indeed very blue.'

He offered no reply. She appeared too young and candid for him to find anything offensive in her words or manner. But he supposed in a place like this and on such an assignment it paid to be suspicious of everybody until their goodwill was established beyond doubt.

She laughed brightly.

'Have I embarrassed you, *señor?* Mama says I must have more modesty, but I always somehow say what I think. This is bad, no?'

'Can be at times.'

'Well, I am as I am, as you surely are, *señor.*' She spread her hands. 'When I see you standing here, I think, I made his bed this morning, I should say hello to this man who sleeps at my house. So I say it.'

She turned to glance back at the women at their work, some of whom were casting dark looks in their direction.

She shrugged eloquently. 'See — they think what I do is wrong also. They will be angry for me speaking to you, as they hate you, or some do. Does it worry you that this is so?'

'I guess they're sore about the shooting?'

'*Sí.*' she answered, facing him squarely again. 'Is it true you slew Lobato?'

'I killed him because he tried to kill me,' he stated flatly. For some reason it seemed important that she understood it had not been murder but self-defence.

'He was a fool!' she said scornfully, surprisingly. 'Another man gone to God because of Toro! I knew that evil one would laugh like a jackass when he heard what Lobato had done, and what happened him because of it.'

'You don't care for Toro, then?' She shook her head and he added, 'I figured he was everybody's hero in these parts.'

'Far from everybody, *señor*. My

mother says he is a vulture and I think the same. Only the fools see him as something else.' She paused, subjecting him to that searching look again. 'Is what they say true? That you have been sent here just to make certain Toro does not escape his hour upon the gallows?'

Stocker drew a turnip-watch from his vest-pocket. Almost noon. He replaced the timepiece and nodded. 'Got to be moving. See you around . . . Carla.'

'Oh, I am sorry . . . I have offended you, perhaps? I should not ask foolish questions . . . Señor . . . ?'

'Stocker,' he supplied. 'Got to go.'

'Then I shall see you again, Señor Stocker? At the house?'

'I reckon,' he answered, moving off.

'*Adios.*'

He looked around once to see her still standing there, staring after him, the gleam coming off the river outlining her body through the thin cotton. He kept walking and didn't look back again.

He entered the plaza and stopped abruptly before the church. The funeral cortège was just drawing away; a single mule-drawn *carreta* followed by fewer than a dozen mourners. The padre, plump, balding and hot-looking walked in front, hands clasped together, face suitably solemn. A rough pine box enclosed the remains of the man who had tried to gun him down — the final resting place of yet another who believed in Johnny Toro.

He stood motionless until the tiny procession quit the plaza before heading on towards the law office. He ignored a bunch of loafers clustered out front of a cantina. But as he drew abreast he heard a whisper; 'Assassin!'

He stopped and stared back. There were five of them, swarthy, dark-eyed and hostile. As one, they feigned innocence, looking up at the sky, one whistling through buck teeth. But the moment he moved on the whispering started up again. He ignored it. There was no time for petty dust-ups, he told himself. That wasn't what he was here for. He walked on.

Then: 'Gringo butcher!'

He went back. No man met his stare.

'Who's got the big mouth?' His voice was like iron.

The men turned, expressions innocent. One said, 'Pardon, señor, you are speaking to us?'

He noted each man was armed, a couple with knives, the others with old revolvers thrust into belt-tops. One sported crossed ammunition belts looped across a scrawny chest. You could feel the hate.

He moved until he had the wall at his back.

'That's right,' he said deliberately. 'I want to know who spoke so I can smash his teeth in.'

The quietly venomous words brought the sting of sudden anger to swarthy faces. A tall man, thin and fox-faced, spoke up boldly.

'I said it, gringo. We just saw them take away the body of a brave hombre. We know you murdered him. We also know who you are and why you are here . . .'

'You're giving me more information than I asked for,' Stocker said, stepping forward. It was doubtful whether the man even saw the fist that whipped out and exploded against his jaw, sending him staggering several feet before crashing into a flower-barrow and thudding to ground, out to the world.

The nearest man snarled and swung a wild blow. Stocker swayed aside. He seized a handful of shirtfront and with a tremendous heave hurled his attacker through the window of the cantina. Glass was still falling as he whipped out his .45 and brandished it in startled faces.

'I'll kill the next man who moves!' he growled. For a moment they appeared undecided. He thumbed the Peace-maker hammer back with a click and every man immediately gave ground, shuffling back.

Citizens stood open-mouthed in the square and upon the plankwalks, staring owl-eyed from the man with the gun to their shaking compatriots.

The one he'd put through the window came staggering out, half-blinded from the blood streaming from head cuts. Had Stocker set out to intimidate the citizenry with further proof of just what breed of man he was, he could scarcely have done a better job.

'Take him off to the medic and get the hell out of my sight,' he ordered. 'The next time I see any of you, step smart out of my tracks or I just might turn mean.'

Meekly the men quickly took charge of their bewildered *compadre* and hurried off. Stocker watched them out of sight before holstering his gun.

People stared after him as he cut across the big square for the law office. Surprisingly few appeared angry, several seemed almost impressed. 'Maybe Toro doesn't have as much support as we figure?' he mused.

He mounted the steps and went inside. Both sheriff and deputy started when he came in and he could tell from their expressions that they had witnessed the incident across the plaza.

'They were begging for it,' was all the explanation he offered.

Both men came to life when he spoke, Kwell going to the window to peer out, Fulton firing up a stogie with shaking hands.

The sheriff said, 'They're some of Santo's bunch. Bad lot.'

'Santo?'

'Toro's sidekick. He's been keeping the outlaws together while Toro's behind bars. He's not as quick with a gun as Toro but is just as bad in most every other way that counts.' His brow furrowed as he turned to study Stocker. 'Those rannies you just tangled with only rode in today. Could be that it was what happened last night that drew them in . . .'

His words trailed off. Stocker stood massaging his knuckles. The sheriff was weak yet, he sensed, likely straight enough. The gunfighter had rarely been afraid, yet still understood what fear could do to a man. He felt almost a moment of sympathy for this middle-aged lawman now, with his sad, sandy moustache and shaking hands.

He reached a decision.

'I'm here on the governor's orders to make sure that Toro doesn't get to bust out,' he declared. 'Seems to me every man jack in this town suspects that already, even though it was supposed to be secret. Anyway, now you've got it from me, first hand.'

'I kinda suspected,' Fulton confessed, meeting his gaze. 'Didn't rightly believe it though. I didn't figure the capital would send anybody down here without first informing me about it. Shows what they think of me, I suppose . . . ' He blinked and cleared his throat. 'So just what are you then, Mr Stocker? A lawman, or mebbe a . . . a . . . '

'Gun for hire? You've got it, lawman. Here's proof.'

He extracted Ballentine's document from his breast-pocket and handed it to the lawman. It stated that one Clay

Stocker was engaged in the temporary service of the Territory and was to be afforded full support and assistance by all peace officers and army personnel in this place if such support was required.

The sheriff scanned it and handed it back.

'Well, maybe the governor knows what he's doing.' He sighed. 'I guess I've seen enough to figure you can look out for yourself.'

'Could be.' Stocker put the letter away. 'I'll see Toro now.'

'Uh-huh.'

Fulton started for the archway leading to the cells. Stocker said, 'Keys.' The sheriff shot him a startled look, but then took down a heavy key-ring from a wall hook and they walked through to the cells.

'There he is,' Fulton said, stopping before a barred door.

Stocker blinked. Instead of confronting some scarred and menacing maverick in this dim light, the prisoner appeared to be little more than a slightly built boy.

This was the terror of the south-east borderlands?

The prisoner stretched lazily like a sleepy cat, puffing on a long black cigarillo. He glanced up insolently at the two men and smiled.

'Stocker, no doubt?' he murmured.

'Let me in,' Stocker said to Fulton.

'Good God, man!' the sheriff protested. 'Talk to him from here. He's — '

'Open the door.'

Fulton shrugged and obeyed. Swinging the steel door open, he said, 'At least hand me your revolver.'

Stocker ignored the request and entered the cell.

'Lock the door,' he ordered. 'I'll yell when I want you.'

The key grated in the lock and the sheriff's footsteps faded down the corridor, leaving the two men alone.

'Sit down, Stocker,' Toro grunted, indicating a stool.

Stocker remained standing.

'Hell, stand then, man.' Toro smiled, dragging luxuriously on his weed. 'Ain't my arches that's aching.' He studied his crossed boots admiringly. After a minute's silence he glanced up again. 'You're not exactly the gabby type, Stocker.'

At first Stocker had reckoned the prisoner to be around eighteen years of age. He could now see that Johnny Toro was several years older than that, maybe twenty-two or three. He was slim and well-built and attired in a frill-fronted white shirt and black *charro* pants made of fine velvet. Handsome with curling black hair, he appeared far too young and too openfaced to be some kind of lethal legend of the borderlands.

Then he met the outlaw's eye and reviewed his assessment. This was no boy, but a man. A dangerous one, or he was no judge at all.

'So, you know why I'm here too, mister,' he stated. 'How come?'

'Toro's got ears everyplace, gun-fighter.' He chuckled. 'Even up at the capital.'

'Well, what you know or don't know

doesn't matter a hill of beans. You're going to hang. That's all that signifies.'

The prisoner gusted a big cloud of smoke across the cell.

'I've heard about you, Stocker. On and off I guess you could say I've heard plenty, over time. You're handy with a gun — I understand that. Tallied up quite a few notches, or so I hear tell.'

He paused and frowned. 'Guess I never figured a gunslinger would turn on one of his own kind.'

'I'm not your kind,' Stocker stated. 'But what is solid truth is that you're a convicted killer and you're going to hang. There seems to be a general feeling that you will break out of here, or that you'll be busted out by others. I'm here to tell you that won't happen. The reason the governor sent me down here was to make sure you hang, but without his having to resort to dispatching a squad of dragoons to guarantee it. He means to convince folks that this is a lawful territory and that just one *hombre* — me — is more than enough to see the law is carried out. You follow the man's thinking?'

'Maybe.'

'Sure you do. Well, now that we've got this straight, a word of advice. I just met up with some of your running dogs . . . and I guess 'dogs' is the right word. But at least they are still alive which they won't be if they have any loco idea of nailing me and setting you loose.'

The prisoner came erect so unexpectedly and swiftly that Stocker went back one quick step, his right hand grabbing his gun butt.

Toro chuckled.

'Relax, gunfighter. When I make my big play you won't even see it coming. Then you'll be dead. But there's no way I will go off half-cocked . . . '

He paused momentarily and Stocker saw every last trace of boyishness drain from the handsome features until he found himself staring into the face of a deadly dangerous man whom it would not pay to underestimate, if he were any judge.

'All right, you stiff-necked mucker!'
Toro hissed. 'You said your piece, now
it's my turn. You and Ballentine don't
have one hope in hell of lynching me,
and I'll tell you why.' He threw both
arms wide. 'The people is why, big shot.
They love me and know I've never done
anything but what's good for them.
When the tax-grabbers were around,
I'd get my *vaqueros* together and we'd
blast a few of those government
blood-suckers and give the money back
to the poor. And when — '

'I'm not hear to listen to you sound
off — '

'And the Rurales, Stocker,' the other
ground on. 'You hears about the
Rurales? They used to come raiding up
across the border from Mexico looking
for plunder. And who ambushed those
bastards and left their bones bleaching
in the sun?' He thumped his chest.
'Toro, is who. Just like you'll bleach if
you don't fork leather and get before
the people here rise up in a way the
borderlands will talk about for ever.'

57

He swung away, running fingers through black curls.

'All right, now get gone, you stinking governor's running dog. Your time is up.'

Stocker was impressed. Didn't show it, but it was so. This man-boy was the real deal. You could smell it, feel it.

Even so, he knew Toro was just whistling in the dark. He wasn't going any place but to the gibbet.

Stocker went to the door and called to the sheriff. Then he turned his head and said softly, 'You'll stretch rope before I ride out. That's a promise.'

Toro flung himself on the bunk and reached for his cigars.

'We're all through talking, big man. Next time it will be gun talk.' He glanced up as Fulton appeared at the door. 'Get him out before he stinks up the place, Sheriff.'

The lawman unlocked the door and Stocker stepped out. He looked back as the sheriff relocked the door. Toro was admiring his fancy boots and lighting up another stogie, a picture of calm and relaxation again. 'You got another visitor, Toro,' the man said. 'You want to see — ?'

Toro looked up with a cocky smile. 'Is that a fact? Well, let's hope it's better company than this one.' The handsome eyes flicked at Stocker. 'Why, it was exactly like talking to a dead man, I swear . . . all the world like gabbing away to a corpse . . . '

His words trailed away in a soft chuckle. Stocker and the sheriff went down the corridor.

He heard a woman's voice in conversation with the deputy as they approached the low archway. Fulton, walking before him, obscured the pair for a moment, so that it was quite suddenly that Stocker found himself staring at one of the most beautiful women he'd ever seen.

'Señorita Trinidad,' Fulton said, 'this is — '

'I already know who he is, Sheriff,' the girl interrupted, her voice modulated yet laced with contempt. 'He could be nobody else but Señor Stocker, hired killer and murderer. You are Clay Stocker, are you not, *señor*? The gunfighter and killer sent here to see an innocent man murdered by the law?'

Stocker made no response, taken aback by her beauty as much as her scorn. He stood staring at her, drinking in raven hair, midnight-dark eyes, the graceful voluptuous figure.

The girl turned to Fulton, who appeared flustered and embarrassed.

'Your new friend doesn't appear to be able to speak, Sheriff. Perhaps he feels ill at ease and inarticulate without a pistol in his hand?' She tossed her head, the long hair making a silken whisper against her blouse. 'I shall go in now, thank you.'

Fulton nodded dumbly to Kwell who walked around the desk towards the arch. Stocker stood before the woman, unaware that he was blocking her way. She tapped her parasol on the floor impatiently.

'Would you kindly step aside?' she snapped. Then under her breath, added, '*Cochino!*' He moved and she went lightly by him, a subtle lingering fragrance of scented young flesh triggering his mind back to some long-forgotten yesterday, before Fort Sumter, before the gun became his friend.

She paused in the archway and whispered so softly that afterwards he was uncertain he had heard right. '*Capón!*'

She was gone with a rustle of silk to follow Kwell down the corridor.

Fulton cleared his throat in the awkward silence.

'Er, you shouldn't be offended, Stocker. She — '

'The hell with that!' Stocker snapped, recovering quickly as always. 'You called her Trinidad. Is she kin of the Don?'

'His daughter. Her name is Maria.'

'And she's visiting Toro?'

'It's a pretty ugly situation, I'll concede. Somehow she met the killer

61

somehow, somewhere . . . nobody seems to know. They'd been seeing one another off and on ever since. Naturally Don Luis is heartbroke about it, tried everything to bust them up, but — '

'Don't sing me any sad songs, Fulton,' the gunfighter chopped in, striding for the door. 'I've heard them all.'

The lawman called something after him that he didn't hear. He crossed the porch and strode off across the plaza, the burning sun striking him like a hammer.

4

Maria

From the private room in back of Armijo's cantina, Stocker could hear the rise and fall in the murmur of the crowd at the bar.

He took out the turnip-watch; just before nine.

He replaced the piece in the fob-pocket, picked up the coffee-cup and was lifting it to his lips when a gentle tap sounded on the door.

He transferred the cup to his left hand, rested his right on his gun-handle and called, 'Come!'

It was one of the serving-girls who entered and began clearing away the remnants of his supper. She asked if he had enjoyed the food, and he nodded. She paused at the door with her tray and coquettishly attempted to engage him in conversation. At the moment, everyone in town was either interested in or suspicious of the gringo gunfighter who'd descended amongst them right in the middle of the most testing period in Mesa Vista's history.

His cold-faced silence stopped her chattering and she went out, closing the door behind her.

He'd bathed and shaved at Donna Salla's before going out, had also changed into fresh rig. He wore dark pants and polished boots with a pale-yellow shirt that emphasized the deep border tan of his face and hands. He felt fresh, rested and satisfied — in his body. He doubted there would be any rest for his mind or spirit in brooding Mesa Vista.

After finishing off his joe he stood and reached for his hat. He opened the door and went down along the narrow passageway past the kitchen, the pungent odour of frijoles and chilis wafting out.

He stepped through the entrance to

the bar and paused a moment. The room was well-filled, with the gambling-tables doing good business and any number of drinkers lining the long bar. Two men in silk shirts strummed steel guitars, a throbbing tango that was both stirring and nostalgic.

Stocker set his hat on his head and made for the batwings, the way clearing before him until one pint-sized Mexican stood wide-legged in his path and glared at him belligerently. The fellow was dirty and drunk with snaggled yellow teeth and bat ears that flapped with the jerky movement of his head.

Stocker halted.

'Move aside or I'll walk over you,' he murmured. He didn't feel aggressive, was just playing the role he always found got best results.

But maybe not this time.

'Pah! I do not fear you gringo,' the runt said shrilly. 'I do not tremble at your step, like these others. For I and all of us know you came to Mesa Vista to see the great Toro die!' His voice rose to a falsetto screech. 'But you will not see this — nobody will see it. Toro shall not die here . . . he will ride free again and smite our enemies. All the territory will see this happen . . . you cannot fight us all!'

The faint murmur of approval swiftly faded. Stocker stood expressionless staring at the defiant wreck before him.

Emboldened, the trouble-maker leaned over. 'Pig!' His foul breath gusted in Stocker's face. 'We will kill you here.' He turned to the room and flung arms wide. 'Are you all *capóns*? Will none of you help me rid us of this evil butcher?'

Calmly, Stocker said loudly: 'Has this man any friends here? Come and get him out of my way before I have to step on him.'

The little man caved in. For he had detected the iron in the gunfighter's voice and was suddenly afraid. Three men rose from a table and took him by the arms. He began to weep. 'Pity and mercy for the great Toro!' he cried as he was booted out of harm's way.

The slatted doors swung closed behind the party as they went out. Stocker made to follow.

'Hey, Stocker!'

His hand dropped to his gunbutt as he swung in the direction of the voice and saw the man who had called his name. He was American, young and hardfaced with a shock of red hair and bitter brown eyes. He was attired plainly but wore two big walnut-butted six-shooters thonged down on each thigh.

'Cherry! What are you doing here?' Stocker frowned.

The man approached with a glass in one hand, the other outstretched.

'Hell, Stocker, is that any way to greet an old pal?'

Stocker ignored the proffered hand. 'What's your business here, gunslinger?'

'Still the same old Stocker.' Cherry shrugged, dropping the hand. 'Heck, old-timer, I'm just passing through. But, say . . . I couldn't help but notice you don't exactly seem to be number one in this lousy old adobe town, do you?'

'That doesn't bother me any.'

'No, kinda figured it wouldn't.' The man frowned for a moment, then said: 'You know — the word is that you're down here to guarantee that Toro geezer doesn't get to duck the hangman? That so?'

'You know it. Why ask?'

'Well, if you want me to level, I figured you'd be way too smart to take on a suicide hitch, man. That feller is big down here . . . I mean real big. They say he's got half the territory scared and the other half eating out of his hand.'

'I've heard that said,' Stocker murmured drily. 'But I reckon it's a load of bull-dust. It's my notion that, apart from the scum who'd back anybody who was against the law, most here seem to feel his hanging is way overdue, only most are too scared to say so. You know Toro?'

'Knew him some back in Lazo Springs. Say, who talked you into this caper anyway?'

'I never tell who I hire out to.'

'Oh yeah ... sure ... old loner Stocker.' The man studied him intently. 'Or mebbe you ain't the same old loner you always used to be? Mebbe by now there's a Mrs Stocker?'

'If there was, would I be telling you, Cherry?'

The gunman smiled quickly but didn't mean it. They were different men in just about every way that counted, bar one. Stocker was a sober loner, Cherry gregarious, hard-living and of course, lethal as a canebrake panther. But the man was about as slick with a .45 as any man Stocker had ever encountered on either side of the law. But that still didn't make him warm to him any.

'Na ... I guess you're still riding single saddle, Stocker. You never paid the dames all that much attention, as I recall ... '

'And you still talk like an old woman full of rum.'

Cherry's gaunt face paled and he

tipped his glass to his lips, studying Stocker over the rim, his free hand an inch from his gun-handle, as usual. The man had earned a rep as a 'jumper' with a gun, meaning if a situation ever just looked like gunplay, he always got in first, fast and usually fatally.

But it stood to reason the man would not go out of his way to tangle with him, Stocker reflected. Sure, Cherry would believe he would win such an encounter. Yet he was smart enough not to be eager to wager both his shirt and his life on the outcome.

Stocker understood why the killer hated him. Cherry hated anybody who might be either his sixgun equal, or even have the edge.

'You still ride mighty high, don't you, Stocker?'

'I've got work to do, pilgrim. *Adios.*'

Cherry watched him move away. He needed to say something to close on a winning note.

'Hey!' he called and the other turned. 'Toro's got more dangerous friends than you've had hot suppers, old-timer! Thought you should know. And you can wager he's gonna get loose, gonna meet up with all his old friends and he is sure as shooting going to come looking for you — big man! You won't stand a prayer.'

The saloon was hushed. Drinkers backed up edgily as Stocker came back slowly.

'I'm here to do a job, Cherry, and I won't back off from seeing it done for any reason. If you've got any notions of getting in my way, make sure you come shooting, boy. And if you want a word of warning, be faster than you've ever been on account of if you're not they might get to bury you and your hero Toro in the same box.'

He left the gunman glaring savagely after him and shouldered his way through the swinging doors.

He paused on the rim of the porch, lighted up and flicked the vesta away.

Once again he was aware of that atmosphere of evil and decay that appeared to permeate Mesa Vista's sultry nights. It was as if the town's menace lay dormant under the sun and came to life only when darkness came down. His lip curled sardonically. 'You must be slipping, Stocker. You never let any town spook you before — so don't start now.'

He nodded in full agreement with himself and went across the plaza.

A bearded loser sat smoking a cornhusk cigarette on the bottom step of the gallows as he passed under its shadow. He kept on until reaching the scrolled-iron gate standing before the home of Don Luis Trinidad.

Light spilled from the windows along the broad veranda as he went up the pathway. The faint murmur of voices and the tinkle of music created an atmosphere of peace and orderly living.

The voices fell silent at the sound of his knock, followed by a woman's quick laugh and the sound of light footsteps.

He removed his hat and stood ready. If this were Maria Trinidad he would not be caught off guard a second time.

The elaborately carved door swung open and she stood before him, her hand flying to her mouth when recognition hit. She wore a blue satin gown that fitted snugly to her waist, scalloped low in front.

Following their first meeting Stocker had convinced himself she couldn't be as beautiful as he imagined. He saw he was right. She was more so, and he realized with chagrin that he was twisting his hat in his hands like some whey-faced kid come calling on his first date.

He made to speak but was silenced by the radiant smile that sprang to the girl's face.

A male voice sounded from the room off the hallway. 'Who is it, Maria?'

'A visitor, Father,' she answered. 'I will bring him in.'

She stepped close to Stocker, that same delicate fragrance he'd first noticed at the jailhouse playing hell with him again.

'You must forgive me,' she said urgently. 'For what happened today. I . . . I do not know what came over me. I acted like a witch and I am so ashamed. Please, do say you can find it in your heart to forgive me?'

He was a man rarely confused, yet was truly confused now. He wanted to remain aloof and cold — he was good at doing both. Instead he found himself nodding his head and saying, 'It didn't happen.'

She rewarded him with a smile, then reached out and took him by the hand. 'I just knew you would be like that. You strike me as a man sure enough of himself to overlook a woman's foolishness and bad manners. Please come in and I shall introduce you to the *patrón*.'

The hallway was wide with Spanish ornaments and tapestries lining the walls, although Stocker saw none of it. It seemed he was only conscious of the girl, and that both angered him yet piqued his intense curiosity.

Two men rose as they entered the big

lamplit drawing-room. One was of medium height with a lean, intelligent face, his companion was portly and self-important-looking.

Introductions were made and he found himself shaking hands with Padre Martinez and Don Luis Trinidad, Maria's father.

'The governor wrote me that you were on your way, Mr Stocker,' he was surprised to hear the impressive Don Luis say with a warm smile. 'He gave you the very highest personal recommendation and asked me to afford you any assistance that is within my power.'

Stocker just nodded. Governor Ballentine had suggested he visit with Trinidad, the leading citizen of Mesa Vista and a man he seemed fully to trust. Momentarily, he wondered whether Trinidad might have released the information that 'the enforcer' was on his way. He immediately discounted the thought. Ballentine would never make an error of judgement like that. If the governor trusted the Don, then that was good enough for him.

He took a seat and the daughter brought him a drink. Tequila. He was impressed. He managed a smile which she returned. He shook his head in puzzlement at his reaction to the girl. Here he was, locked into one of the most potentially dangerous assignments he'd ever undertaken, yet at the smile of a beautiful woman he appeared to be reacting like . . . well, like some saloon dude, like Cherry.

Conversation proved remarkably easy with these people. The padre was jovial and cordial, while Don Luis told him of his early struggles to build his fortune and how he was fighting now to ensure he kept it.

Stocker had come here tonight mainly to discuss Johnny Toro and his pending date with the hangman. But the company made no mention of the killer, so neither did he.

Yet not for a single moment was he about to overlook the fact that Maria Trinidad was rumoured to be both a friend and supporter of that back-shooting little scut.

Did that mean she was loco? Or might Toro have a lot more to him than had showed at first meeting?

So ran his thoughts as the padre made his goodnights and was shown out by a silent servant. But his thinking ran treacherously awry as she bent over him to refill his glass and her breasts were momentarily at eye-level.

The loveliest woman he'd ever seen? Most likely. But what in hell that might have to do with who he was and why he was here, he couldn't begin to guess.

'The good padre seemed just a tad uncomfortable with me around, Don Luis,' he remarked, making sure he looked at the man and not his daughter now.

'Ah, Martinez is much burdened with many troubles these days, Señor Stocker. I suppose ever since Toro came to power here it has been increasingly difficult for men of the cloth, like the padre, and men of wealth and possessions, such as myself. Of course he would not approve of your profession, yet he would still realize you have come in the interests of the town's well-being, that your presence is highly necessary. But he would have to be apprehensive about what negative effects your coming might have upon Mesa Vista . . . whether you might increase or diminish the tensions and violence we expect to experience as the execution date grows nearer.'

'Well, like they say, you can't make a cake without cracking eggs.'

He said it deliberately, watching them both. No point in trying to convince them that he was anything other than what he was. He'd arrived wearing a Colt .45 which he would be expected to use and use effectively should big trouble break here. That was what he did.

But Don Luis took no offence. 'Maria, would you kindly have cook brew us some coffee?'

'Schemer,' she said banteringly. 'I know you want to be alone with our guest for a while.' She ran her fingers through her father's silvery thatch before going out. 'Cream and sugar, Mr Stocker?'

'Black, thanks. And you can make that Clay, if you would.'

The richly appointed room suddenly seemed cold and dreary the moment she disappeared. The gunfighter looked a question at Don Luis.

Don Luis turned sober. 'You of course know about Maria and this murderer?' Stocker nodded and Don Luis went on. 'It is terrible, a shame and a great worry. I reared her with all the love and care in the world, denied her nothing. Then overnight she falls in love with one of the worst possible types you could ever wish to meet. *Dios mio*! Her mother would be stricken had she lived to witness it. I have tried everything, reasoning, pleading, even threatening. All to no avail. Nothing I say has the slightest effect. She is even so blinded by this man that she doesn't believe him to be the wretched outlaw everybody else knows him to be.'

Stocker rose and moved about the room. Leaning against the marble fireplace, he said, 'Why don't you move out? Take her with you and quit Mesa Vista?'

Don Luis rose, pale-faced now. 'No! I shall never do that. I came here as a poor young man and wrenched wealth from this grudging earth. This is my home and I shall not be driven from it by a coldblooded little *renegado* like Johnny Toro!'

Stocker put a hard look on the man. 'Then you will just have to live with the situation and hope for the best.'

'No, no,' protested Don Luis. He crossed quickly to Stocker's side, his manner suddenly conspiratorial. 'There is one way out, I believe. Maria is an only child, spoiled and impulsive, and I am certain this affair with Toro will prove to be but a passing whim. But what if she were to become interested in another man . . . ? Yourself, perhaps?'

'What?'

'Hear me out,' Don Luis begged. 'I saw Maria watching you earlier. She is drawn to you, I can tell. You'll pardon me if I say she seems to exhibit a weakness for dangerous men. Do you think . . . would it be preposterous to ask you to see Maria whenever you can, to seek her company, flatter her if you must. Who knows where it might lead?'

Stocker was at first stunned by the man's suggestion, then angered. And yet when he saw the pain and worry in the older man's eyes, he held back a sharp retort. He knew it must be painful for the man to make such a proposal . . . he had likely swallowed a lot of pride to plead a favour of a man like himself.

'You're grabbing at straws,' he said quietly. 'I'm not exactly a maiden's dream, you know. Likely I have more blood on my hands than Johnny Toro. I am a gunfighter, man. I kill men in the line of duty. That's the reason I'm in Mesa Vista. You have got to understand that and get shook of any crazy ideas.'

He went to the wall where his hat hung on a hook, took it down and moved for the doors.

'Wait!' pleaded Don Luis, trailing him. Then suddenly Maria stood framed in the doorway, barring his exit. She held a silver coffee-set and her eyes showed surprise.

'Señor Stocker, you must not leave before you have had coffee. See, I brewed it especially for you.'

He stared at her. Her luscious young prettiness and the angelic mysteriousness of her personality struck deeply into his gunfighter's remoteness.

He dragged his eyes away from her and glanced over his shoulder at her father, who shrugged and smiled ruefully.

'Can you resist her, Señor Stocker? Most find it almost impossible to do so.' He gestured. 'Do please be seated.'

He was trapped. It almost felt good. He replaced his hat on the hook, resumed his seat and Maria set about serving the coffee in fine little silver cups.

Eventually he relaxed and leaned back, the small cup looking even smaller in his strong, long-fingered hand as he watched her fussing over cream and small, sweet-tasting cakes.

He found his eyes drifting over that faultless face, the satin smoothness of bare shoulders, the deep cleft between her breasts as she bent over the service.

If only he were younger, he found himself half-dreaming . . . and in his mind's eye saw a Stocker before the guns came to dominate his life and shape his character.

As though from a vast height he looked back at his own young self sadly, affectionately . . . his youth and joy in living . . . and then Chancellorsville, Gettysburg . . . Bull Run . . . a million graves . . .

By the time it was all over he had discovered he was better with a gun than any man he had ever faced . . . a battle-hardened man of just twenty-three.

He'd felt old even then. He felt twice

as old admiring Don Luis's daughter . . .

'Mr Stocker?'

'Yes?' he muttered, then realized Maria had been speaking to him. 'What was that?'

'You were miles away. You seemed to be dreaming. You will have Father and me believing we must be poor hosts.'

'No . . . I was just thinking. Go on.'

The remainder of the evening passed agreeably with easy conversation, good wine and later a fragrant supper served by a maid.

Later, Don Luis excused himself, pleading tiredness. The gunfighter and the girl chatted on for some time, but by the time he was leaving he'd brought himself back down to reality. Gunfighters did not fall in love. He'd barely known any like himself who had even married. What life could it be for any woman whose husband left her each morning with no certainty that she would ever see him alive again?

Then they were standing side by side

in the shadowy portico surrounded by the sweet evening odours of roses and flowers, a bloated moon hanging in the black sky over the plaza.

He moved to the steps.

'*Señor.*'

He turned and she was in his arms. Incredulously he felt the moist lips on his mouth, the hands about his neck, the pressure of her body against his. Then just as swiftly and surprisingly she was gone, leaving him staring after her.

He touched his lips and half-smiled.

He had no notion of what had provoked that kiss, yet he was glad of it. For it had reminded him that she was just an innocent child who should be protected, as he would protect her if needs be.

It had been a charming evening yet, as soon as Stocker started across the *placita* in the sinister Mesa Vista night, the girl was gone from his thoughts. For no matter how relaxing that couple of hours had been, this was reality. The hard-edged reality of the stark gallows passing on his right, of the old Spanish church where two men had been given a requiem mass, of the weight of the gun on his hip.

And yet he cocked his head a little to one side as if listening to a distant guitar . . . and he could still smell the roses.

5

The Unknown

Two days passed swiftly, two blistering, brassy days, two long and sultry nights.

Tension grew like a live thing and violence simmered just beneath the surface in Mesa Vista.

Men gathered in groups at the cantinas or upon the *placita* to gossip and make dark vows, and their eyes were worried, fearful or ugly.

Johnny Toro lounged in his cell, smoking long cigarillos and trading jokes with the deputy turnkey while Sheriff Tite Fulton brooded in his office, swallowing cheap liquor and starting at every unexpected sound.

Fear, hatred, suspicion, uncertainty. Clay Stocker encountered them all whenever he prowled the square with the big gun riding his hip, and it seemed not a man of them dared meet his gaze squarely.

And while Toro lay on his bunk admiring his boots, every daylight hour brought the thud of hammer and the rasp of saw as the gallows neared completion.

The word going around was that the governor having decided that the convicted killer must be executed here upon his own bailiwick as a warning to his many admirers and followers, that big day would only be announced when the gallows job was completed.

Rumors persisted that the Toro gang would show up any day to rescue Johnny from the hangman, that Santo, his feared *segundo*, would never see him abandoned in his hour of peril.

At first Toro had merely laughed at the ominous sounds of industry from the *placita*, then had ignored them.

But over recent days he had sometimes dozed, to awaken abruptly with the thud and rasping seeming to hammer in his ears . . . only to realize that it was the middle of the night when the whole lousy town was asleep!

At such times he might get up and start in raising hell to draw the lawmen, then attack them, listing the tortures and ignominies he would inflict upon both after he won his freedom and before he subjected them both to the death by disembowelment he'd promised every day since the day of his capture.

He was able to scare them and that made him feel strong. For a time afterwards he might pace his cell with a lithe and lively step, and whenever somebody visited with food, tobacco and threats against his captors and promises to set him free, he would sing and boast and feel every inch the Toro of old.

He would rather hang twenty times over than have any man of them know of those times when he awoke at night and could still hear the carpenters at work — even when he knew they had all long gone home.

While gunslinger Cherry spent his days and nights drinking and gambling, watching the young girls go by swishing their hips at him — and waited patiently for Stocker to get himself killed.

Many held Cherry in awe for it was an open secret that he had ridden with Toro on and off, and was therefore suspected of being here in Mesa Vista to take part in the long-predicted freeing of the county's favourite butcher-boy. Or so some figured.

Cherry was in town, Santo was expected to show up any moment, Toro's wild bunch was reported to be lurking someplace close by now. These were the possibilities but only Cherry was real at the moment — reassuringly so to the Toro admirers.

His past exploits with the Colts, both real and fanciful, were given a wide airing and Cherry would preen and strut in the limelight and sometimes treated them to an exhibition of his amazing gunmanship in back of the saloon.

Occasionally he encountered Stocker, who passed him by without a word, the last of the straightbacks with those steely eyes flicking every which way and that big shooter at his side. At such times Cherry might spit a curse — or if it was a bad day — come down with an attack of the shakes.

He knew he could beat Stocker and therefore found it hard to understand why that bastard scared him at times.

Then he would reassure himself by concentrating on 'the bunch'. He and Toro had reason to believe the condemned man's gang would soon make it up the trail from Mexico and should then be quickly assembling at the hideaway in the remote hill country at Chino Gulch — or at least should be by their calculations.

Killing time, Cherry rode out to make doubly certain that Oxtail ranch still held that big herd out on its south range just ten miles from town, waiting to begin the trail-drive up to the railhead.

They had plans for that mob of

longhorns. Big plans.

There had been an incident when Cherry was drunk and started in bad-mouthing Stocker and assuring admirers and sycophants he could whip the governor's gun blindfold with one hand tied behind his back. His companions vanished like ferrets down a rabbit-burrow when Stocker walked into the midnight saloon in a black mood over something. Having caught a few words of invective relating to himself, the gunfighter straight away braced Cherry, who was smart enough not to accept a challenge in the liquored-up shape he was in. Stocker accepted this argument, then knocked him cold with a right hook to the jaw, which still ached days later.

Cherry had a high-paying assignment in the northwest awaiting him after Mesa Vista. He was to kill a gambling dude who'd run off with a railroad tycoon's young wife. The tycoon was growing impatient but would simply have to wait. Everything must wait until

Stocker was dead, Toro freed, and Mesa Vista had ceased to exist.

* * *

Governor Ballentine reread Stocker's latest wire one last time before screwing it up and throwing it into the waste-basket.

The message was terse and to the point — exactly like hearing Stocker speaking. The governor was now convinced that Mesa Vista was a genuine powder keg of tension and rumour ready to blow, with only one genuinely reliable man down there capable of keeping the lid on.

Briggs and other palace advisers had pestered Ballentine to dump his plan to have Mesa Vista conduct the execution without help from the capital, but the governor stuck to his guns. Those vermin must learn to respect the law, he contended. And they might never get to do that should he be forced to wheel in the cavalry every time some outlaw was scheduled to shake hands with the hangman.

'But what if your plan fails, darling?' his lady wife had asked unhelpfully just the previous night. 'Rumour has it that this awful Toro person has vowed to escape and destroy not only the jailhouse but the entire town. News of a disaster like that could carry all the way to Washington. And where would we be then?'

The Territory's premier citizen hadn't deigned to answer this rhetorical question at the time, and dismissed it from his thoughts now as he returned to his desk.

The first document awaiting his signature, and marked Urgent, was an official authorization for two cavalrymen to accompany one Ethan Haley, official hangman, to Mesa Vista.

He dipped his pen and hesitated, then quickly signed his name. He sprinkled drying-powder on the paper and called: 'Mr Briggs. Get this letter off at once.'

* * *

Two days passed and there was more than simply menace poisoning the air of Mesa Vista . . . something else had been added.

Nobody seemed certain what it might be. But at times, and for no apparent reason, men would suddenly fall silent in saloon, office or out on the streets, heads cocked, listening and with their questioning eyes fixed upon one another . . . and there would be nothing to hear and after a time they would mutter embarrassed '*adioses*' and go their separate ways with puzzled faces.

Or perhaps a woman might suddenly grab up her baby and press it to her breast in a fiercely protective embrace, not knowing from what evil she imagined she was protecting it.

In the church upon the *placita*, more candles than ever before were burning upon the altar of the Virgin of Guadalupe, while outside, eyes were drawn to the crucifix upon the bell-tower and many a churchgoer, blatant sinner, or worse, might be seen making the sign of the Cross on shoulders, foreheads and breasts before passing on by.

It was now only a matter of days before Toro was scheduled to hang . . . and the ancient soothsayer on Alamo Avenue kept warning dolefully that these would prove to be the darkest days of Mesa Vista.

★   ★   ★

Her dark eyes were huge in the lanternlight. 'But why have they not come, Johnny?'

'They will come. Do not worry about my brave *compañeros, chiquita.*'

'But the time grows so short.'

'*Sí*, very short for the governor, these stinking lawmen and that *pistolero* from the capital. Toro shall not sleep until all are dead . . . and until he rules all the lands south of the capital, for he loves the poor ones and they love him!'

'I worry about Clay Stocker, my

Johnny. He comes much to my father's house. I think . . . I fear he seems invincible.'

'Do not worry about Stocker either.'

'But I do, my darling. I worry desperately day and night. Is there not something I can do?'

'You can believe in me.'

'I do . . . more than anything, I do.'

'Then nothing can harm us.'

★   ★   ★

Stocker halted outside Toro's cell. The killer was breathing deeply, fast asleep with the afternoon light fading slowly from the barred room.

He turned away and went back down the passageway to the office.

He heard the clink of glassware as reached the archway and glimpsed Sheriff Fulton furtively closing his desk drawer when he entered the office.

Even without the glazed look clouding the lawman's eyes, the pungent whiskey smell in the room would have given him away.

'You figure that will help any if trouble breaks?' Stocker growled.

Fulton looked discomfited at being caught out. He attempted an apologetic smile, but something caused him to turn somber again.

'Not 'if', gunfighter. You . . . you said if trouble breaks. Won't be any if about it, I know that much now. It'll be when, man, not if. When!'

Stocker's stare was cold and contemptuous. The sheriff was weak. He had no patience with weakness in another.

'So, what's the latest rumour?' he demanded sarcastically. 'Chief Wildhorse bringing his war party a hundred miles to burn us all in our beds? Or has that story been traded in for something better?'

'The band . . . Mr Stocker . . . that gang . . . '

'Oh yeah.' Stocker moved to a barred window to gaze out over the square. 'Toro's gang. I'd kind of forgotten about that. How strong are they at the moment? Fifty? Or was it five hundred?'

He turned to confront the lawman, his stare as hard as the rifle-bore of a Winchester .32.

'Toro's been in that cell three weeks, Sheriff. Doesn't horse sense tell you that if there was a band — even a band of two — they'd have made their move by now? What would they be waiting for? Riddle me that.'

But Fulton refused to be reassured. Sometime during the past week he'd grown convinced that all the rumours were true concerning the prisoner and his imminent escape; now his only comfort was the bottle.

He cleared his throat and croaked, 'How's Toro doing back there anyway?'

'Asleep.'

'We fret and he sleeps. How does he do it?'

Restless and tense, Stocker crossed to the door and stood leaning against the jamb, watching a huge sunset drain away in the west like blood.

The gallows were close to completion and the hangman was on his way from the capital, yet Johnny Toro slept like a baby.

It didn't figure.

Not for Clay Stocker it didn't.

He doubted any man living could sleep during daylight hours while his death by hangrope was imminent, unless . . .

That 'unless' had been nagging at him all day. For the only notion that even came close to explaining the killer's nonchalance had to be that the man knew he was not going to swing.

If that were the case, then it could only indicate that Toro truly believed he was to be set free.

But how and by whom?

The Mesa Vista *Tribune* liked to report in its pages that the 'Toro Gang' was 'twenty to thirty strong'. He'd questioned the editor on this claim but the man had proved unable to substantiate his assertions. Other rumours of planned escapes sounded even less convincing.

Stocker would not be giving any of them brain-room if that boy-man in there hadn't continued to doze on tranquilly like someone without a care in the world.

*   *   *

He paused on sighting Don Luis's daughter on the square, and stepped back behind an abutment.

Maria Trinidad was walking slowly towards her home. He saw her pause and turn her gaze back towards the jailhouse, then move on. He waited until she had vanished inside before he stepped out and made his way to Donna Salla's.

Characteristically direct in his relations with others, Stocker had to admit that that lovely young Maria threw him completely. Everyone admired her, the father doted upon her, while Stocker himself had her figured as about the finest-looking woman he'd ever seen. And yet she was said to be crazy loco about a convicted killer!

Work that one out, gunfighter!

He continued on down the lane past Armijo's and entered the little court leading into Donna Salla's. As he stepped inside the stables he was greeted with a contented grunt by the sorrel, now restored and well-grained. 'You're doing just fine, Pablo,' he complimented the stable-hand, and tossed him a coin as he left.

He crossed the court and climbed the outside stairs to reach his room. He doffed his hat and shirt, shaved carefully and sluiced cold water over his chest and arms.

A light footstep sounded outside.

He dropped the towel and faced the open door-way with the Peacemaker in his fist.

''Allo, Stocker.'

He lowered the weapon as Carla Salla swung in with a swish of skirts and perched herself on the end of his bed.

'Mmm . . . muscles.' She smiled. 'I thought you would have them.'

He wasn't much for smiling, but she could usually make him do so. Her attitude towards him was different from anybody's in town. She was friendly, unafraid, frank and at times a reliable source of information.

He reached for his shirt and tossed her a box of vestas.

'Make a light,' he grunted.

'No, not yet. This is the beautiful time of the day, so we will enjoy it a little longer, no?'

He nodded as he tucked his shirt into his pants. He had a hunch the girl might have some sort of crush on him, or maybe thought she did. He was flattered but that was about all. He was too tied up with Toro and the upcoming execution to think about romance. Tonight, as usual, her company was welcome yet he remained moody, an ongoing sense of tension and uncertainty working on his nerves.

After a while she said, 'You are silent, Stocker.' She never called him anything else. 'And you look tired.' She patted the bed beside her. 'Rest. You do too much, carrying the town on your back.'

He frowned and then complied, the bed creaking under his solid weight. He stared out through the small window at the gathering gloom, unable to cheer up. Here, as it was upon the *placita* or at the saloon, the jailhouse or walking by the river, you could feel the tension and uncertainty. It was out of character for him to feel affected, yet he reckoned the situation he found himself in here to be unique.

She reached across and patted his shoulder. He made to draw away but for some reason remained unmoving.

'Why do you do it all?' she asked at length. 'The work, I mean. Sooner or later you will be killed, if not here then somewhere else. You know that to be true. So why, Stocker?'

'It's the only thing I'm good at.'

'I do not believe that. I think you are an *hombre* who could do anything, if you wished to do it.'

'Maybe in your eyes I could. But

you're young and haven't lived. I reckon you might see me as something I could never be.'

She smiled.

'So, the great *pistolero* believes he can read the mind of a woman also?'

He rose quickly but she slid from the bed and linked her arms about his neck. For a moment he held her against him but then unclasped her arms and held her away.

She protested but he turned his back on her and put a match to the lamp on the wall bench.

'You are afraid of me,' she accused, sounding like a woman with an age of experience. 'Why so? You do not fear the dangerous ones such as Toro and Cherry, why a girl who washes clothes in the river and helps her mother clean the rooms?'

He studied her. She was making good sense, he supposed. He was also thinking how lovely she looked in the lamplight, before his thoughts drifted to someone else.

It was as though she could read his mind. 'She is beautiful but not for you, Stocker. No, do not look surprised. You know I mean Maria. I have seen the way your eyes follow her. But she is crazy for Toro, which means she is simply crazy.'

She was saying things he likely didn't want to hear. Stocker turned and moved towards the window. As he did, the glass exploded into a thousand pieces and a heavy slug whipped past his face to thud into the wall behind with the deep-throated bellow of a heavy rifle sounding close by.

In one blurring motion he seized the girl, hurled her to the floor then flung his body across her. The Peacemaker filled his fist as another bullet whipped through the window and shattered a water-jar.

'Stay down!' he ordered. 'Just stay down.'

'Whoever it was must be on the roof across the alley!' she panted, as he sprang to his feet and went lunging for the door.

'Reckon you're right.' He'd already figured the shots could have only come from the roof, as there were no windows opposite his own, just the high plank wall of the barn.

He also realized that the only way down from that roof was the plank stairway rising from the alley.

The rifle boomed a third time as he seized the handle and reefed the door open. Bent double, he streaked for the nearest passageway window, touched off a shot at the shadowy figure he glimpsed across the way. Instantly the sniper disappeared and moments later he heard the sound of rapid steps upon the outside stairs.

He reached the landing. Without hesitation, he vaulted the railing and dropped ten feet to the ground. The girl rushed out in time to see him dart across to the barn wall and flatten himself against it close by the corner where the stairway began.

The dim figure of the man rushing down the stairs warned her to duck low a moment before a bullet gouged the wall behind her.

It seemed plain that the dry-gulcher hadn't seen Stocker streak across the alley to the barn, for he kept coming down fast, cursing in Spanish, boots stuttering on the steps.

The rifleman hit ground level and Stocker hit him, coming round the corner of the building in a tigerish rush that saw the rifle jolted from the man's grasp.

As he staggered and tried to regain balance, Stocker backhanded him so hard he was flung against the wall with blood running from his mouth.

Stocker waited for him to fall. He didn't. He was much bigger than Stocker had anticipated, and tough. He proved just how tough when he launched himself off the wall, lowered his head and hit Stocker in the chest like a battering-ram, driving him out into the light as the area began to fill with onlookers drawn by the sounds of violence.

Stocker's boot-heel snagged on something and he was falling. Big hands locked about his throat as he landed hard on the flat of his back. His right knee came whipping up, sunk inches deep in the man's groin. His attacker groaned in agony but realized he had far more to moan about when Stocker sprang erect with the agility of a catamount, kneed him under the jaw then seized him by both shoulders and smashed him into an adobe wall with all his strength.

Stocker stood back and let him fall like a plank, face smashing into the hard-packed earth of the yard.

He lay unmoving.

But Stocker was moving. Fast.

He came in with a vicious kick to the head and would have kicked again had not the girl reached him in time. She seized his arms and shook him with all her strength.

'Stocker, enough, *hombre*. Do you wish to kill him?'

The look in Stocker's eyes said 'yes'.

But it was quickly gone. His rage had been against himself for almost allowing himself to be killed, or worse, for being responsible for innocent people dying.

'It's OK,' he panted as the crowd gathered round the still figure. 'Anyone know who he is?'

Heads shook. He appeared to be a stranger. But as Stocker bent to haul him up into a sitting position, a bearded carpenter came forward and said, 'I reckon I seen him once when Johnny and the boys got back from a raid on the border . . . ' He paused a moment, studying the unconscious figure. He nodded. 'Yeah, he's just a herder as I recall, but he sure took to Johnny and seemed to like what he said about getting rid of the outsiders and running the town for the plain folks . . . like Johnny was always saying . . . '

He flicked his eyes at Stocker. 'Small-timer, I reckon. But I guess it goes to show just how deep feelin's go here, mister.'

His chest still heaving, Stocker

glanced around. The faces that looked back at him were a study. Some appeared shocked by the violence but a large number appeared resentful and almost hostile.

He nodded to himself as though in acknowledgement of a truth he'd been trying to avoid. A man could get killed here. The governor had packed him off here to prove that he would not be panicked into making a bigger thing of Toro's execution than he wanted it to be. Up until this moment, Stocker had believed he had what it took to carry out any assignment. But when the man in the street could get so worked up about the situation here as to try and kill a man, that had to be a warning a man would be a fool not to heed.

He bent again, seized the still unconscious figure, slung it over one shoulder and strode towards the gate.

The mob trailed him out, then followed him along the street with others joining the procession as it went.

'What are you doing?' cried Carla,

running after him.

'Don't horn in,' he snapped. 'And get back inside. No saying if this mightn't start something big.'

She halted and he kept on for the plaza, toting the dry-gulcher as easily as though he were a child. The throng at the street mouth gave way as he approached, wide-eyed as they joined the bunch trailing him into the square.

All the oil-lamps had been lighted by this and there was a sizeable crowd already gathered to see him stride swiftly to the centre of the square, where he paused to dump his burden at the foot of the all-but-completed gallows.

'Hear this!' he yelled. 'This yellow scum just tried to kill me. I know why and so do you. He's still alive, and he should be dead. I let him live . . . giving him back to you. But I'll tell you straight now. From here on in, if any citizen makes one move to stop me doing what I came here to do, I'll kill him and anybody with him.'

He deliberately holstered. 'Any takers?'

No response. He was frightening and they were suitably frightened.

He appeared taller than before as he span on his heel and strode away, tall and invincible.

But he knew he wasn't. He was still one man against hundreds and now he knew what he must do.

★   ★   ★

The thud of Stocker's boot-heels down the side street slowly faded and immediately the babble of voices began to rise on all sides.

There were men rushing across to peer down at the still unconscious gunman, others gathering in knots gesticulating and arguing, citizens leaning from high windows, some shocked, some alarmed, most at least a little fearful at what they had seen and heard.

Standing alone on the porch of a dry-goods store, Cherry nodded almost admiringly, smiled mirthlessly.

What a stage act! he thought sarcastically, yet with an edge of bitterness. For Stocker had saved his own neck then bluffed a whole town in a way that simply had to impress. He shook his head. Only Stocker would pull a stagey stunt like that. Only he could, most likely.

He cursed and went searching for a drink.

★　★　★

The *bandido* scout managed to wade some twenty feet out into the rain-swollen Rio Moritomo before being forced to retreat to the bank where the band waited.

'Has gone down, *amigos*,' he reported back to the bunch. 'Maybe by this time tomorrow we can swim the horses across.'

'No maybe,' came the curt reply. 'This time tomorrow we cross. Should we delay one hour longer than that, we might only get there in time to cut Johnny down from the gibbet.'

Dark heads nodded. Tomorrow night it must be.

* * *

'So, Don Luis, you understand why I have to do this now?'

'Perhaps you would explain one more time, Señor Clay?'

'Sure. Look, I figured from the start the governor was taking too big a risk in insisting that Mesa Vista take care of Toro's execution without any real outside help. His reasoning might be sound but the numbers just don't add up. I'm alone here — one man. The governor is relying on the lawmen to stand strong, but they're both made of jelly. The town's at least three-quarters behind the renegade, and what happened to me tonight shows they are getting worked up and could come after me in a mob.'

'I fear that might well be possible, my boy.'

'Well, they won't get the chance. I'm

big headed enough to believe they won't have the guts to come after me by day — numbers notwithstanding. But a man has to rest, so they could maybe take me by night. That's why I aim to camp up in that wooded gulch above the plateau until Toro's ready to mount that gibbet, then I'll come to face them down by daylight, whether his bunch shows up or not.'

'Those are still terrible odds, Clay. Are you sure — ?'

'Dead sure,' he said firmly, rising. 'Needless to say you're the only one who'll know my whereabouts, so . . . '

He put a finger to his lips in an age-old gesture, then quit the big room. Don Luis sighed and settled back into his chair. His daughter, concealed in the heavy drapes by the piano, brushed away a tear and at last realized what she must do.

For Johnny Toro.

6

Jail Time

Santo stared across at the jailhouse, sucking on a cheroot, a one-armed killer with the face of a hawk, and at the moment, a worried frown.

'Nothing!' he hissed to the man at his side. 'No word from the band, nothing from Johnny. Time is our enemy so we must do something . . . '

'Like?' queried the other.

Santo stared around desperately. A passer-by smiled fawningly, for Santo's standing as Johnny Toro's right-hand man lent the one-armed *pistolero* great status in some quarters.

'Hey, you — Quiller!' Santo called. '*Sí*, you. Come here. You would like to see Toro free again and not swing from the governor's rope, no?'

'*Sí*, Santo.'

Santo tugged a wad of bills from his shirt-pocket and handed it across. 'Then go and buy a gun . . . no . . . many guns. Then meet me at the saloon in one hour.'

The man grinned and trotted off. Santo felt his henchman's stare upon him. 'What about the herd *amigo*?' he asked. 'Toro has long planned to use the herd to teach these vermin a lesson they will not — '

'Johnny planned to make use of the cattle when he got out, Otero. We cannot use it as a weapon of revenge while he is in that accursed jail . . . he might be also killed.' He turned and started off. 'Come, we must do what we must do.'

★　★　★

Johnny Toro paced his cell like a caged animal. Despite his vanity he'd not shaved that day. His black thatch was tousled and his hands clenched and unclenched continuously as though he was grabbing invisible gun-handles.

He ached for the touch of gun steel, the stink of cordite, the death-rattle of a man dying at his hands.

His rescue was way overdue.

That was the cause of his explosive mood tonight. He'd expected Cherry or Santo to make their play long before this. Of course his chain of supporters had passed the warning to him that the bunch had been delayed by floodwaters to the south. He also realized that Cherry couldn't be expected to buck both the lawdogs and Stocker without backing, deadly as he might be.

He halted and sleeved his mouth.

Stocker!

That was the one ace he hadn't reckoned to run up against in the enemy's deck of cards. Maria had kept him posted on most of what that guntipper was doing day by day, even what he could be thinking or planning at times.

She'd won Stocker's confidence; he reckoned she could charm Lucifer himself if she set her mind to it. But he would need more than her information, a booze-hound sheriff and his own lethal skills and leadership if he were to survive.

He needed his handful of hellions who'd die for him and he needed to be free. And not tomorrow, right now!

He pressed his face against cold metal bars and tried to relax over long minutes. Then the colour drained from his face and he could hear it again — that phantom tapping and sawing of the gallows-builders even though he full well knew every man Jack of them would be snoring in their beds at this silent two-in-the-morning hour!

He was hearing things again. The situation was getting to him.

Biting his lip, he whirled away from the bars and hugged himself against the chill. Someone was going to pay for this. Then, clapping his hands against his ears, he made a correction. Everyone would pay!

★ ★ ★

Stocker stood beneath the cottonwood gazing out over the lights of Mesa Vista, the mountain quiet and resting behind him. There was the sweet smell of grama grass on the air, the faintest of breezes stirring the leaves in their sleep.

Off to one side, hidden in a grassy cleft, the sorrel cropped contentedly. The animal was well-trained, never requiring picketing, always ready to come at a snap of his fingers.

Beyond the rim the ground fell away some fifty feet to the wide plateau before sloping away gracefully to the rangeland below.

And further out gleamed the sprinkled lights of Mesa Vista.

He'd spotted this hideaway on a routine ride the previous day and had come in to inspect it, already anticipating that he might need to pull out of town by night.

Despite Don Luis, the two lawmen and also a surprisingly wide level of support from the town itself, he'd grown increasingly aware of the danger of his operating virtually one-out in the town, particularly when it came to sleeping.

Already there'd been an attempt upon his life, so he'd eventually decided that if anybody else had the same notion in mind he would have to be prepared to take his chances up here where Stocker believed he would hold top hand.

His horse was the best watch-dog ever.

There was a cave in back of him. It was deep and dry and contained his bedroll and provisions for man and horse. At least he could sleep in peace here away from sidewinder guns and mad Mexicans. A man needed his rest . . . he fully expected things to get far worse before Toro walked on air.

He walked to the edge of the rim and peered down towards the trail far below.

Then he raised his eyes and stared out over the darkened distances to the south.

No sign of Toro's bunch, as yet.

Naturally he'd heard all about them, how many there were and how ferocious and blindly loyal they were to that *hombre* in Fulton's jailhouse.

Well . . . maybe there was a band who could be as menacing as some claimed. He would play that card if and when it was dealt. So far, the Toro bunch seemed just so much talk.

Not so Cherry.

His eyes narrowed. He seriously doubted a class gun like redheaded Cherry could have simply wandered into Mesa Vista by chance at this specific time. He would bet good money that the shootist was linked up with Toro in some way. That, he took seriously. He was confident enough to believe he could edge that blood-nut in a shoot-out. But with the Cherry breed, you could never be dead sure. Maybe the man didn't mean to gunfight him, rather to do him in any which way he might. That was a prospect to disturb anybody, even a pro like himself.

After making a last check on the drowsy sorrel he entered the cave. He'd already spread his bedroll and now, by the light of a vesta, took one last look around the cave before turning in.

He removed boots and gunbelt in the dark and drew a single blanket up over him. He had packed a cushion of pine-needles beneath his bedroll and the comfort was almost the equal of his bed at Donna Salla's. With the Peacemaker snug beneath his headrest within easy reach, he gazed out past the cottonwood in the moonlight until he slept.

The night's hours slipped by. In the grassy cleft, the high-shouldered sorrel stood hipshot with its weight on three legs, head drooping. A foraging badger waddled by silently, searching for fieldmice. The moon waned and paled . . . a brooding pre-dawn hour of total darkness . . . then dull gray washed up silently from the east.

Stocker muttered in his sleep, turned over restlessly and shifted the position of the arm he'd been sleeping on, half-awaking for the moment.

Abruptly he found himself staring into the blackness above him, the hair on the back of his neck lifting. The dregs of sleep slid reluctantly from his mind and he recalled dimly that there had been a sound . . . some sound from somewhere that must have been unusual enough to feather his sleeping senses . . .

He sat up and peered at the dim outline of the cavern mouth.

Nothing.

Night and day were struggling for supremacy out there, the bulk of the cottonwood looming dimly against a lightening sky.

He massaged the back of his neck, wondering what he had heard — or imagined. There was no identifying the sound, yet some stubborn sense warned him that there had been something.

He stiffened. Rising out there some fifty yards downslope was a moving figure. It was a man!

He was on his knees in an instant,

cocked sixshooter in his fist.

'Hold it!' he shouted, and the dim shape froze. 'One step closer and I'll drill you dead centre!'

The figure remained motionless a moment longer, standing silent and ghostly, close to the cavern mouth. He appeared to be draped in some sort of cape and the gunfighter could not determine his size. Then there came a sudden rustle of movement.

'I friggin' warned you!' Stocker bawled. 'Just stay put . . . I'm coming out . . . '

His shout was engulfed by the roar of a gun and a streak of light came lancing out from the figure's darkened bulk. A bullet snored by him to clatter and whine against against the walls in back of him like a demented insect.

He ducked low beneath a second shot, locking his sights upon the crouched figure of the gunman. The bellow of the Peacemaker almost deafened him within the confines of the cavern and he saw the man reel back, his gun exploding harmlessly into the earth. Stocker's next bullet chopped the man down but before he hit the earth he'd driven a third shot into the body.

Lips curled back in a silent snarl Stocker leapt erect, cursing and breathing hard with his ears ringing painfully to the percussion of the shots. He reached down and plucked three fresh shells from his gunbelt and refilled the empty chambers as he went forward.

He was no longer worried about the man on the ground. He knew where his bullets had gone. But he was still wary, for there might be more than just one. Approaching the mouth, he crouched against cold stone, every sense alert for sound or movement.

A full minute went by. Five. Nothing.

He emerged from the cavern. The light was growing stronger by this and he could see there was nobody else upon the slope below.

Breathing more easily he straightened up fully and turned his attention to the motionless figure sprawled in the dew-damp grass. The man appeared

127

small up close, the body swathed in the heavy cloak. As he moved to within a few feet, he halted abruptly, a sudden chill coursing over him . . . there was something wrong here . . . the shape of the body . . . a pale, slender hand protruding palm upwards, delicate fingers curling towards the wrist.

The closer he drew the deeper his sensation of alarm and uncertainty. Small dainty feet and a cloud of midnight hair fanned over the grass.

It was a woman!

As a hammer thudded in his brain Stocker dropped to his knees, his trembling hands reaching out. They touched soft flesh. For an eternal moment he was frozen, unable to think or move. Then with sudden desperation he turned the body over, face to the sky.

It was Maria and she was dead.

★　★　★

The swimming horse came surging up out of the still swollen river, struggled for long moments to find its footing, then kicked and clawed its way up on to the sandy riverbank, the rider lashing it every inch with his quirt.

Carlos shivered in his saddle and looked back at the dim shapes of horsemen on the far side.

'Is OK!' he shouted. 'Keep on the high side of the boulders and you must only swim the little bit now! Come, do not be afraid, *muchachos*.'

A great gout of white spray shot into the air as the next horse and rider plunged into the swollen waters and began to thresh their way across. As soon as he had safely passed the half-way mark the remainder of the outlaw band put their mounts to the flooded Moritomo until all were safely secure on the river's steep northern banks.

'No sign of Santo,' the leader said, still breathing hard as he glanced about.

Heads nodded in agreement. Johnny Toro's lethal lieutenant was nowhere to be seen in this brooding nightscape where the hellions had expected to meet up with him.

'I think he must be in the town,' another opined, shivering. 'For we are very late, the hour for Toro grows close . . . ' He paused and nodded emphatically. '*Sí*, either Santo is in the town or else he is with the herd . . . '

Heads nodded in agreement. Ever since heading back north to help Toro, his hellions had known about the herd at Oxtail ranch, and the role it was to play in Toro's escape and vengeance against the town.

'We shall stop by Oxtail, and if Santo is not there we will find him in Mesa Vista. *Hola*!'

At the shout Toro's henchmen galloped north, racing the sunrise.

7

Gun Alone

Beyond the panes of the naked window the evening dusk was gathering.

The objects and artefacts on the walls of Don Luis's study slowly lost their clarity, the tapestries and swords, the Inca relics of beaten silver . . . all slowly losing their identity with the fading light . . . and for the first time in two hours the man in the deep leather chair stirred.

As though waking from drugged sleep, Stocker leaned forward stiffly and blinked about him, listening to the stillness of the great house and the distant, angry babble from the plaza.

He rose and moved to the window overlooking the enclosed courtyard where a servant was watering flowers from a long-stemmed can.

Wherever he looked he found reality as opposed to the fog of shock that had held him in its grip until now. He found himself suddenly capable of thinking back over the terrible hours since he'd reached the house of Don Luis.

Much was vague, yet he clearly remembered Trinidad's incredible courage when he'd seen his daughter, then his offering Stocker sympathy upon hearing his story, where the gunfighter had anticipated rage and condemnation.

And later still, the mob screaming and howling outside, demanding retribution over the 'murder', whipped up by Yaqui Santo demanding his blood.

He had sat unmoving in the study, only half-hearing the clamour, scarcely caring if they should break in and drag him off to some brutal death. It was then that Don Luis had gone out alone and ordered the crowd away, and from force of long habit and respect they had obeyed him in the end, their consideration for a father's grief stronger than

Santo's fiery harangue.

The door opened quietly. He turned and saw Carla.

'Stocker?' She was unable to see him in the now-dark room.

'Yeah?'

'Shall I bring in a light?'

'I don't give a damn.'

She disappeared and he remembered she'd been with him all the time in the study, seated across from him, not talking, just being there.

Carla had been prepared to remain with him through that endless afternoon into the night and for as long as it took, if it would help a man she'd loved from the moment she had first sighted him at the river, seemingly an eternity away now.

She had simply stayed and prayed that some of her young strength might help to draw him out of the cage of pain that held him captive. She had been elated to see him coming out of it at last, the old familiar clarity returning to his eye.

She returned to the room now toting a large, wrought-gold lamp. She placed it upon a table, then went to the windows and drew the shades. She turned to study him and her face lighted up. He was now watching her, seeing her, the awful emptiness she had seen in his eyes throughout the day virtually gone.

''Allo, Stocker.' She smiled, remembering how this greeting always appeared to amuse him. He didn't smile; she had never seen him genuinely smile. But there was something new in his eye there, a hint of gratitude, perhaps?

'Hello, Carla. What time is it?'

'Almost eight.' She crossed to his side. 'You feel all right now, I think so?'

'Sure . . . all right.' He swung his arms to restore circulation, coming out of it faster now. 'What's going on outside?'

'There is much talk and great anger. You heard Don Luis talking to them just now?' He nodded and she went on. 'That was Yaqui Santo trying to goad them into action. He and a few scum are out there among the people now, working them up against you, against anyone who might oppose them. But although many may yell and curse your name, I think they fear you too much to try and do you harm. It is said that the rest of the Toro gang has been somehow delayed, otherwise they might well be here now, and that would be bad.'

She paused with a frown, then added, 'There is an *Americano* also speaking against you.'

'Cherry.' Stocker sounded sure.

'You know him? Is he an enemy of yours?'

'Isn't everybody?' he muttered bitterly.

'No,' she said softly, 'not everybody.'

He rose and stood looking at her, studying her closely with a kind of perplexity. Footsteps sounded beyond the room and moments later Don Luis entered.

The man was pale and the lines in his face seemed to cut far deeper than before. Yet he was immaculate and elegant as always and when he spoke the voice was calm and controlled. Stocker admired him as he had admired few others.

'The end of a terrible day, Señor Stocker. You are all right in yourself?'

'Yeah,' he replied. 'Yourself, Don Luis?'

'No pain lasts for ever. This much I have learned in my long life. You would like some refreshment, perhaps some wine?'

'Nothing, *gracias*.' Stocker grimaced. 'I guess there are some things a man knows liquor just isn't going to help.'

Trinidad moved to a side table and selected a goblet. He frowned at it thoughtfully. 'There is much danger in town for you tonight, *señor*. I can feel it. I strongly advise you leave after full dark. Not even the governor could blame you.'

'And leave them free to bust Toro out just when it suits them? Not a chance.'

Don Luis filled the goblet and fixed

him with a steady eye.

'To help ease the pain I know you must feel, I must be honest with you, my friend. Concerning Maria, I mean.' He sipped his drink and his gaze was distant. 'She was always both the loveliest and strangest of daughters. From childhood she was reckless with odd likes and dislikes. As she grew towards womanhood her choice in friends and suitors seemed to grow ever stranger. I lost count of the times I was forced to intervene to retrieve her from some unwise friendship or liaison. Toro was simply the latest and by far the worst of these . . . '

He turned to look at Stocker squarely.

'I see now that, sooner or later, what happened last night would surely happen. You did not kill my daughter. Whatever she felt within herself, whatever strangeness or mystery, was responsible for that.'

Stocker nodded. '*Gracias*, Don Luis.' That was a huge thing to hear from a father's lips. It lifted some weight from his shoulders, but not all.

'But what does it all matter now?' The older man sighed. 'I realize that there can never be law and order in Mesa Vista now. It was all a dream and may well remain so for another hundred years. Whether Johnny Toro lives or dies will be of little consequence now. The dark forces have triumphed . . . I was a fool to think I might help keep them at bay.'

'You don't really believe that. Nor do I.'

Stocker went to a far corner of the room with a firm step. His Colt lay on the carpet with smudges of paint on its surface. A gouge mark in the ceiling indicated the point where the weapon had struck when he'd hurled it violently from him several hours earlier. He retrieved the sixgun and, rubbing it clean on his shirtsleeve, came back slowly across the room.

'I will see this through,' he announced, studying the weapon in his hands. 'If I don't it means that those men which this thing killed . . . everybody it's killed . . . died for nothing. It's a bad thing for anyone to die for no reason . . . '

His voice trailed off and for a time he appeared mesmerized by the lamplight shimmering silently off the Peacemaker's long barrel.

He glanced up at the older man, his gaze clear and focused again. He hesitated, searching for the right words.

'Don Luis, it isn't much, but if I ever get to ride away from this town I want you to know I won't be taking this gun with me . . . not any gun. I'll be looking for another way to live my life after this. Like I say, that isn't much of a gift. But just maybe it might make up a little for what happened to Maria . . . me quitting the trade might seem like some good coming from her dying . . . '

It was a long uncertain moment before Don Luis replied.

'I will keep your pistol . . . and shall always know what it means to us both.' He touched Stocker lightly on the shoulder. '*Adios* and good fortune,' he murmured, and walked from the room.

Stocker rammed the sixshooter back in its scabbard and reached for his hat. Action was what he craved now. Danger, opposition, uncertainty; they never failed to ease his inner conflicts.

He turned at Carla's light touch on his arm.

'Do what you have to do without guilt, Stocker.' Her eyes searched his face. 'Do not hate yourself too much. Maria loved the assassin enough to kill or to risk death for him . . . perhaps she even wished to die? For I do not believe Toro could love her or any other woman with all the hate that is in him, and I think she also knew this in her heart . . . so maybe for her to die is not so bad . . . '

'Maybe,' he murmured, half conceding that Maria must surely have suspected that a killer like himself could not be accounted for by any woman. 'Maybe you're right. But I can't figure how she knew where to find me up there.'

'You had told Don Luis where you were going when she was hidden behind the curtains. I saw her leaving the room. She must have overheard.'

He shrugged, feeling the darkness closing on him again. He realized that he shouldn't talk of her too much yet, must clear his mind of all diversions if he expected to survive whatever lay ahead.

He made for the doors.

'Where do you go now?' Carla asked anxiously.

'Armijo's. Everyone knows I eat there at night. If I don't show they'll figure I've either cracked up or turned yellow, and I learned a long ways back that a dog'll always snap at running heels.'

'You may be going to die.'

He looked at her standing by the table, the soft light upon her face. Despite the voluptuous figure and woman-wise ways, he had always thought of her as a girl. But now she appeared every inch a woman, with a woman's love in her eyes. He knew he would never forget the long, terrible hours she had spent with him that day, sharing his agony and helping him recover.

'*Adios, mia cara,*' he heard himself say.

He saw the astonishment and sudden smile at his unexpected words, heard her whisper, '*Vaya con Dios,*' as he strode out to face the town and its hatred.

★　★　★

The cantina clock had just struck ten when the slatted doors crashed open and Stocker came through to stand wide-legged and rake the room with his eyes. In his right hand he held a Winchester repeater rifle and a second sixshooter was thrust behind his shell-belt.

Armijo's was packed with more men than he had ever seen in the place before. The tables, jammed close together with gamblers and drinkers seated around them, were littered with cards, chips, bottles and glasses. Men lined the full length of the bar while here and there the brief and gaudy costume of a percentage girl showed brightly against worker's denim and Mexican *charro*.

Cigar smoke hung thick in the air and the oil-lights gleamed off glass surfaces and staring faces.

Stocker's face was pale and tight, his cold eye seeming to fall upon each man in the room in turn, showing nothing, fearing nobody.

That first weighty silence eased as many looked away, and here and there a glass was raised.

He stood his ground for a full minute, silently inviting the reckless word or the challenge which didn't come.

Eventually the guitars started up again, fresh drinks slid across the bar, the murmur of voices slowly welled up all around the room.

Only then did he move, making his

way slowly down the length of the bar towards the rear of the cantina.

Familiar faces showed amongst the crowd. He saw the little Mexican with the great, floppy ears who'd abused him earlier, now quickly avoiding his eyes. He paused a moment before Cherry who leaned lazily against the zinc-topped bar, nursing a glass of pale Mexican rum. The gunman raised his glass in mocking salute and Stocker moved on.

Then he sighted Tite Fulton.

The lawman occupied a quiet corner of the bar and had his shoulders hunched high as if trying to conceal his face. Stocker crossed directly to him and stood there for a long half-minute before Fulton was forced to turn to face him.

'Hello, Stocker.' He grinned amiably. He was drunk, stupid drunk. 'Join me in a li'l old drink?'

'Get back to your office and sober up smart, Fulton.'

A look of mock indignation replaced

the sheriff's sodden grin 'Tarnation, a man's entitled to a little old drink, Stocker. Ain't no harm in that, eh, boys? What do you say — ?'

His sentence was cut short as Stocker reached out to seize him one-handed by the shoulder and with a heave sent him stumbling, almost falling towards the door.

'Get!' Stocker ordered. 'Now!'

Fulton appeared bewildered. His moustache quivered and he looked like a man coming apart. He turned clumsily and staggered for the doors, bumping men and tables as he went. A man laughed derisively. 'Better go lock yourself up, Fulton — you rumpot!'

General laughter followed the lawman as he half-fell out of the cantina, but the mirth dried up as attention returned to the gunfighter.

He let them feel the weight of his eyes before moving to occupy a vacant stretch of bar, leaning his back against it and facing the room.

Suddenly a man scuttled from a

corner and slipped furtively through the doors into the night — a man with sixguns, floppy sombrero and crossed bandoleers of ammunition slung across his chest. One of Santo's dogs, Stocker guessed. Likely gone to tip off the leader. He shrugged and turned his back upon the lot of them, walked unhurriedly to the single rear door and passed along the passageway leading to the private room where he customarily ate.

Armijo himself came to wait on him. A little roly-poly Mexican, the saloon-keeper tonight wore a harassed look, with sweat running down chubby cheeks into the thick rolls of fat encasing his neck.

'*Mucho disturbio*, Señor Stocker.' he lamented.

'Yeah, Armijo, plenty trouble all right.' He gestured. 'I don't want food tonight.'

'No food?' Armijo appeared perplexed. He glanced out through the door towards the barroom, then returned his attention to Stocker.

'You take all the risk to come here this night, yet then you do not wish to eat? You may well need your strength. *señor*. You must surely know that Yaqui Santo is in town tonight. I feel it only fair to warn you that most people say this wild one will slay you and then take Toro from the jail. Both have much hatred against Mesa Vista for permitting Toro to be taken here and held for so long under the shadow of the gallows. It is even said that Toro has ordered Santo to slay you over what happened to the girl.'

He flinched before Stocker's suddenly cold stare. He spread chubby hands. 'I only repeat what they say, *señor*. I do not wish for you to die.'

'I believe you, Armijo. And thanks for the warning.' He lifted the rifle into sight from beneath the table. 'I'm ready for Santo, Cherry, Toro . . . whoever. Tonight's as good a time for a showdown as any.'

'But the evil ones have men . . . and who knows how many from the town would support Johnny Toro?'

'I doubt there'll be that many when the chips are down. Most of the big talkers and biggest boozers around here don't want any part of me. They're yellow and know I won't back off. Sure, they hate my guts. But hate doesn't make a man bleed. And any geezer who raises a hand against me tonight knows he's got a good prospect of dying.'

His words so unemotionally delivered seemed to chill the little cantina-keeper.

Armijo spread his hands. 'But what if you should be wrong and all the town stands against you . . . ?'

'Then I'm a dead man.'

'May the Virgin protect!' Armijo breathed fearfully and rushed from the room at the sudden sound of breaking glass.

★   ★   ★

Smoke trickled lazily from his cigarette. Stocker took another deep draw, exhaled. Good tobacco. He leaned back in his chair and lifted one booted foot to the bench, a picture of comfort and indolence even if that impression might be far from the reality.

He'd spent a silent hour in the room alone with his guns and his thoughts, his mind as cool and clear as always whenever violence threatened.

Ever since Santo had come to town to raise the level of unrest, he'd suspected they would have to come face to face sooner or later.

Rumour had it that Toro's main bunch had been long delayed in reaching Mesa Vista down south in some place. If they should arrive, he reckoned the real trouble would start then.

He wondered if that time could be tonight. Toro would have to be in desperate haste to bust out of Fulton's jailhouse by this time; it was drawing perilously close to noose-time now. Toro, Santo, possibly Cherry — the bunch — and God alone knew how many more backers and supporters

they might attract — all would realize
that the governor's gunman had to be
taken out of the game before they could
feel safe in Mesa Vista.

He cocked his head suddenly.

There was a lessening hum of voices
filtering back from the barroom now
— the scrape and shuffle of many feet
was increasing.

So he sat staring at his hands resting
on the table and considered the
possibilities.

What was going on out there now?
And did he really give a damn? He was
one against however many hated his
guts here, and this was likely just as
good a place as any to make a stand.

He wouldn't run. He'd never run
before and wasn't about to change
. . . not when his life might well be
about through.

He realized he'd never felt this way
ahead of trouble. It was almost as if he
had no real interest in the outcome. He
understood why and wondered if the
enormity of Maria's death might not

rob him of that deadly edge he'd always been able to rely upon whenever death breathed close.

He would soon find out.

For it had now grown ominously quiet at Armijo's cantina.

No music and laughter sifted through from the bar now. The shuffle of feet and the hum of voices had ceased. Stocker methodically rechecked rifle and sixshooters for the final time then cocked his head sharply at a peal of sudden laughter, the sound of a woman's voice. Now light footsteps were approaching along the corridor.

He cocked the rifle deliberately and trained the muzzle squarely on the door. The handle twisted sharply . . . and Carla rushed through.

'Stocker!' she gasped. 'They're out there waiting for you, *hombre*!'

She was flushed and breathless, with one sleeve of her blouse ripped out at the shoulder. With one hand she held the torn edges of her dress together.

He was enraged. He fought the

feeling down. *Never hate your enemies too much, Stocker, remember? It affects your judgement.*

'What the hell are you doing here?' he growled, getting to his feet.

'I was on my way home from Don Luis's when I saw all the drinkers hurrying away from here. When I looked in I saw that Yaqui Santo and some bums had assembled . . . were waiting for you to appear. I came in to warn you . . . ' She indicated the torn dress. 'Santo did this. He seized me and tried to kiss me, but I am strong, and got away. Another *bandido* tried to prevent me coming in here but Santo made him release me. He said to tell you he is waiting for you and that . . . and that . . . '

'What?'

'He said your mother was a whore.'

'Uh-huh.' He moved forward beneath the droplight, rangy and hard-faced, no hint of either uncertainty or emotion evident in the lean planes of his face. 'Any towners backing them?'

'Perhaps just one or two. The rumour still is that their bunch has not come. But these men have been drinking and Santo would make them want to fight. All have weapons.'

'Cherry with them?'

'No . . . not him.'

That was something, he reflected. His chances against a bunch of drunks could not be all that good, he conceded. But with Cherry backing their play the odds might prove way too heavy.

And then the pride in him — the gunfighter's unquenchable pride — said: *Could make the difference . . . not will . . .*

He motioned Carla from the room and trailed her into the corridor. Passing a small spy-window he glimpsed a hairy-headed *bandido* slouched lazily against the back bar. The man spotted him and turned his head to call to someone out of sight.

'After I pass through this door, girl, bolt it tight behind me and don't open it for anybody. You and the Armijos will be safe enough back here. These scum are only interested in me.'

He reached for the door.

'No!' she begged. 'They will kill you. I could not live if y — '

'Bolt it!' he snapped and strode on through to make his way past the scullery where he caught a glimpse of the kitchen staff huddled fearfully upon the floor.

A moment later he entered the barroom and closed the door in back of him with a bang.

There were five men spread around the big room at intervals. They were dirty, mean-eyed saloon boozers and back-street bums. But they had guns, were fired up on tequila, and had Yaqui Santo calling the shots. That made them son-of-a-bitch dangerous enough.

Stocker stood motionless before them and focused all his attention upon one man. That man was smiling at him fearlessly like a wolf, and had an empty shirt-sleeve pinned to his shirt front. Santo.

Toro's *segundo* spoke but Stocker didn't catch what was said. Didn't need to. His face showed nothing as his flickering gaze assessed every man in the big room, noting their exact positions. He glanced up at the tiny windows high upon the west wall, the four big oil-lamps that hung on pulley chains from the ceiling . . . and suddenly knew exactly what he would do, and how it must be done.

He heard the bolt slide home in the door behind him.

Good. She was safe.

To his right, thrusting out some six feet from a side wall, stood a bench around waist high which was used as a half-way point for plates of hot food coming out from the kitchen. His gaze flicked back over the gunmen and lingered imperceptibly upon those four lamps again before settling on Santo, who now watched him keenly.

'So, at last I come face to face with the *hombre* who has spread such fear in Mesa Vista,' Santo sneered, exuding some brand of lethal assurance. 'Why, tonight you do not appear such a fearsome *hombre*, Señor Stocker. Is that not so, brave *amigos?*'

He wasn't deceived by the heller's outward nonchalance. Not even with the numbers his own way could Santo be that relaxed. But instinct warned him that the one-armed gun was ready to give the signal for the slaughter to begin. He would not give him that chance.

Now! he told himself. But even as his hand was starting down the batwings banged open and Fulton lurched in, blinking in the sudden light.

It was totally unexpected, but Stocker sought to take instant advantage of it.

'Not a moment too soon, Sheriff!' he shouted loudly. 'Got the posse with you like I ordered?'

Fulton froze like a deer caught by a blinding light, slow to grasp what he'd blundered into.

All heads but Santo's swung towards the intruder as he reversed and grabbed at the doors again — sensing the danger and taking to the toe.

His henchmen diverted by the incident, Santo alone whipped Colt from leather and brought it up to firing level in one electrifying motion.

But Stocker's Winchester was already beating heavy thunder across the room.

He wasn't shooting at Santo.

Instead his first snap shot exploded one of the four overhead lights. He instantly dropped to one knee, lightning-fast and instantly blasted a second.

He dropped belly-flat an instant before Santo drilled two slugs at him, the sounds coming so close together they sounded as one rolling shot.

Stocker rolled violently to get beneath a table which leapt and shuddered as Santo's lead slammed into it.

Other guns were chiming in by this time. But Stocker wasn't there any longer. A headlong dive had taken him to momentary safety beneath the heavy oak table, where he lay on the broad of his back squinting along his gunsights up at the third light — ignoring the thudding bullets ripping huge slivers out of his protective cover.

He got another yellow blob in his sights and squeezed off two shots, the Winchester bucking hard against his shoulder.

Showering glass rained down and the big room was darkening as ragged drunks rushed forward attempting to line him up in their gunsights, while a desperate Stocker kicked from one position to another with an agility inspired by pure desperation.

Only one light remained in the smoke-filled room now.

Suddenly he leapt up, showing his upper body as he triggered at nothing. Immediately he dropped belly-flat again. With the drawn fire yammering above him, he now propelled his body towards the left corner of the protruding bench, then swung partially out from cover to train the rifle upon the last surviving light.

More wild lead whistled close but the rifle was almost raised to firing position again. He gasped and flinched as a bullet scored white-hot across his left shoulder. The drunks were shouting and cussing like maniacs now. He steadied the gun with dust and grit flying in his face from a slug that whacked into the oak table, almost too close.

He fired, missed.

More lead came whistling through all the smoke and clamour. But they couldn't see their target and he could.

He triggered again, twice in rapid succession, and the room was plunged into instant darkness with just a faint outside glow frosting the front street windows.

Acrid cordite stink filled the interior and gunsmoke stung searching eyes. All around him, florid cursing blended with booming gunfire, the thud of lead upon adobe, the crash and tinkle of breaking glass.

Stocker knew what he must do.

Discarding the rifle he fisted his Peacemaker and hurled himself away from the protection of the bench. Shots responded to the sound of his movements but they were still directing their fire to where he'd been moments before, not where reflexes and desperation had taken him now.

His groping hand found the leg of a chair in the darkness. Coming up on to his knees, he hefted the chair and flung it hard away to the left. His ploy was rewarded by a terrific outbreak of fire that shattered glassware and set riddled walls trembling, creating massive damage to Armijo's bottled supplies in the wall behind the back bar.

Forward he slithered on his belly now. Fire-flashes pin-pointed the position of the nearest enemy and he could hear the rasp of the invisible man's breath. When the man fired again the gunflash illuminated his ugly face, angled upwards. At close range Stocker's .45 slug left a small hole when it smashed through the drunk's chest and a huge crimson wound when it erupted from the middle of his spine.

Confusion and chaos reigned in Armijo's cantina . . . but Stocker now held a lethal edge. For he knew every man still alive in this room was his enemy, whereas the hellions couldn't know whether they were shooting at him or at one of their own.

Gunblasts, howling bullets, screams of rage. A wounded man sobbing in pure agony briefly passed against the dimly lit front windows. Stocker's cutter spoke again and the Mexican was driven bodily through a shimmering shower of shattered window-glass to strike the outside porchboards with a sodden thud that seemed to jar the whole building.

Hefting a busted chair, Stocker hurled it into the shelves of bottled supplies. Under cover of the ensuing clamour he crouched low and darted forward.

Crashing blindly into a sturdy table, he grunted in pain and instinctively flung himself on to the floorboards as bullets homed in on the noise he was making.

Face down, breath rasping painfully in his chest, he listened to men stumbling about in blind darkness before a man howled in pain, wounded by one of his own.

The odds were lessening but were still stacked against him.

Sudenly he found himself close by a window. This offered his only possible escape. He knew this because someone had set himself up close by the batwings from where he would be in position to shoot anyone attempting to escape that way, be he friend or foe.

So — just the one hope.

Bunching his body into a ball, he suddenly stretched out fully in a desperate headlong dive and torpedoed headlong through the window with crossed arms protecting his head, smashing through the glass, his momentum carrying him clear through before slamming him upon the walk outside with brutal impact upon one shoulder; then he kicked desperately for the edge with a slug in his leg.

Sprawled upon the ground and concealed from sight from the cantina by the overhang of the porchboards, he waited in a lather of sweat, chest heaving, fingers busy with bullets and revolver.

It was momentarily quiet from within, with sinuous wisps of gunsmoke writhing from shattered windows.

Risking a quick glance above plank level, he stiffened as he gimpsed the pale outline of a face peering from a broken pane. Reacting instantly, he snapped off a shot and was rewarded by a cry and the crash and clatter of a tumbling body.

Wild curses were followed by sudden silence. In the unnatural stillness Stocker waited, sprawled upon his back, head angled upwards and forwards, a sixgun in either fist now.

The odds had been cut significantly. Two men dead for certain, he calculated: the one he'd drilled inside and the other spread-eagled lifelessly where he'd crashed through the plate window. He suspected at least one other had been wounded by his own men and was hoping the man at the window he'd just clipped might be mortally hit.

He hadn't escaped unscathed himself, but reckoned he'd gotten off lightly, considering.

His leg and shoulder hurt plenty; the warm blood was sticky to the touch. The shoulder wound appeared slight but the bullet in the lower leg had lodged securely and painfully there.

Movement sounded from the darkened interior, then came the sounds of strident voices followed by the thump of boots and shoulders against wood. They were trying to smash open the rear door, he realized. He settled down to wait. There would be no knocking down that sturdy teak *puerta* with its iron-bracketed hinges and slide-bolt, so he figured. Nor could he see any chance of desperate men seeking escape through the little high windows overlooking the alleyway.

There came a continuing mumble of voices from within, then more argument.

Stocker dropped lower when a storming volley came ripping through the front windows.

The gunfire from the cantina ceased abruptly and shadowy figures came scrambling wide from the alley behind the cantina, blasting sixgun fire in a wild and reckless volley.

Stocker had them in his sights.

Twin guns bellowing, he brought one figure down heavily with a second clutching his belly crashing atop the other immediately.

A third man made it all the way to the street at the far right end of the gallery only to die in mid-stride when two bullets thudded into the back of his skull simultaneously.

The fourth and last figure to emerge from the alley flung his sixgun away and raised his hands to shoulder height. But Stocker was shooting too fast to stop. Again his sixshooters spewed fire and death and the figure doubled over clutching his mid section and crashed down into the street.

Breath tore in Stocker's throat and his heartbeat didn't begin to slow until he realized it was over.

Coming erect, he first limped left, then right, examining the still figures.

Santo was not among them.

'Come on out, Santo!' he hollered, his voice booming in the shocked silence of the street. He was losing blood from the leg wound, felt the first flutter of weakness.

'Come in after me, *cochino*!'

'The hell I will, greaser!'

Yaqui Santo's voice quavered with hysterical venom as he unleashed a torrent of invective from the dark and smoking interior, before lapsing at last into silence.

Screwing his head around, Stocker glanced past the ominous shape of the gallows to the law office. He envisioned Toro in his cell, likely standing upon his bunk trying to see out, heart thudding expectantly, waiting for his rescuers to come set him free . . . for not for a moment had Stocker believed this whole thing was not about taking him out in order to set the killer free.

No sign of a lawman, of course. But of course 'lawman' was too big a word to fit either sheriff or his deputy.

Minutes dragged by.

By this time the square was stirring and frightened faces appeared at darkened windows all around the plaza. Towners held no terrors for the gun-fighter; he kept a wary eye open for Cherry, yet the fast gun failed to appear.

Suddenly Santo's voice again; 'Will you swear not to shoot if I surrender, *pistolero*?'

'For the time being, I will,' he called back. 'How many left?'

'Myself and one other. He is wounded.'

'Then send him out first . . . hands up!'

After what seemed a long time the man pushed out through the doors of the darkened saloon with Stocker's gunsights frozen upon his scrawny chest. He held his hands high and blood stained his right flank. Staggering, he made his way down the broad steps and stared at Stocker with horror and fear.

'Lie face down with your arms extended!' Stocker rapped. 'One move'll be your last!'

'*Sí . . . sí*,' gasped the gunman and obeyed.

One to go.

'Your turn now, Santo!' he yelled.

He heard dragging footsteps and Santo opened the bullet-shattered batwings and stepped out on to the gallery. He paused to stare about at the sprawled and silent figures about him, then focused on Stocker.

'Too many men die,' he said hoarsely.

'You should have thought of that before.' Stocker heaved himself upright and stood flexing his injured leg, gun rock-steady in his hand. 'Step down, you son of a bitch!'

His one arm held shoulder high, the *bandido* stepped down slowly and deliberately, eyes cunning and cruel beneath his yellow sombrero. Stocker limped across to him and ran hands over chest, waist, arm and legs, then stepped back. He jerked his gunbarrel towards the jailhouse.

'Move!'

With a shrug the Mexican turned and Stocker took one step after him when a whisper of sound from the cantina brought him whipping around. He glimpsed a gun barrel trained upon him from underneath the slatted doors. Instantly he hurled himself aside as the hidden weapon spewed vivid yellow fire. The bullet snored past his face like a demented bee. Stocker struck ground with his left shoulder, fanning his gun hammer with his right hand, conscious from the corner of his eye as he did so that Santo had taken off like an even-time runner.

Twice the concealed gunman's sixgun thundered but his aim was lousy. Stocker fired with brutal precision until the gun thudded to the boards and he could dimly make out the dead face in back of it.

He leapt to his feet and ran — the hell with the slug in his leg! By this time Santo had made fifty yards towards the gallows. At the sounds of pursuit, he reached his hand up on to the brim of his big hat and brought it down instantly, clutching a revolver.

Stocker cursed his carelessness as gunflame belched from Santo's fist. He ducked and weaved and returned the running man's fire. But Santo's long legs ate up distance at an astonishing rate and in a lightning instant he had disappeared beyond the the church.

Head swimming, leg afire with pain, a heavy-breathing Stocker made his way across to the rear of the church. He cursed. The heller had gone.

But as he turned slowly away he was at least able to tell himself that the big attempt to bust Johnny Toro out of jail had failed.

The *placita* seemed to dance in his vision as he turned back towards the saloon, took half a dozen uncertain steps, then fell forward on his face and lay still.

A full minute went by before people slowly emerged from hiding, eyes wide at the carnage they had witnessed. First to reach Stocker's side was Carla.

8

Escape!

Hangman Ethan Haley and two Territorial guards reached Mesa Vista the following day at noon. Expecting to find a town of fermenting violence and danger, the party instead encountered calm and order. Admittedly, few townsmen were to be seen upon the broad plaza, and as a consequence their arrival was greeted with little fuss or surprise. Accustomed to hostility on account of his grim profession, Haley was at first astonished then relieved at their low-key reception.

The party first stopped off at the jailhouse where they presented their credentials to Deputy Kwell. Fulton was currently sleeping off the effects of a drunken spree aggravated by the shock and terror of almost becoming involved in a desperate gun battle overnight.

The party inspected the prisoner in his cell while Kwell afforded details of the carnage.

Haley anxiously asked after Stocker's condition upon learning he'd been wounded. The hangman had only accepted this assignment with just two cavalrymen for protection after receiving assurance that the governor's gun would be on hand to ensure his safety.

He was assured that Stocker was already up and about and had been put up at Don Luis's house.

The three walked their mounts across the square and hitched them to the rack alongside Stocker's sullen sorrel.

They found Stocker seated upon the pillared veranda, watching them as they came up the paved pathway.

He nodded coolly to Haley who introduced his escort as O'Brien and Trask. While Stocker acquainted the hangman with the present situation in the town, the governor's cavalrymen stared in awe at the gunfighter, who was the talk of the town after taking on an entire bunch of Toro's riders, the survivors of which had vanished into parts unknown.

Stocker advised the group to check in at the hotel, from which point Haley could complete his preparations while the cavalrymen alternated between guarding the hangman and keeping one eye upon the jail.

Haley sat staring admiringly across at the grisly new gallows and started chatting about the coming event as though it was a festival or some kind of grisly peep-show. Stocker shut him up promptly, and shortly afterwards the trio left for the Paradiso Hotel.

Stocker massaged his leg, feeling the thick strapping under the denim pants. He'd honed his knife and cut the slug out himself at Don Luis's house. He'd come close to passing out from pain and loss of blood but half a beaker of twenty-year brandy had sustained him. Carla had then cleaned and dressed the wound after which he'd slept. The treatment was repeated when he awakened and now his leg had improved sufficiently to support him.

The shoulder crease was painful but not serious and he figured he'd gotten off lightly. Characteristically he didn't dwell upon the dead men, now awaiting burial at the undertaker's. He had fought and won and that was the end to it all.

He would have given a lot to take Santo out of the game, for that one was surely the real McCoy, his talent as a shootist somewhere close to his own.

He had no notion where that lean-gutted shootist might be right now.

Of couse he figured Santo might have simply withdrawn, pulled out and quit. On the other hand, he could just as easily be — even at that very moment — sitting someplace taking a quiet jolt of tequila and finalizing his new plan to save Toro from the rope.

Only time would tell.

Stocker remained on the veranda

until mid-afternoon. Don Luis sat with him a spell and they talked of many things, freely and openly in the way of men sharing mutual respect. The gunfighter knew he would think often of this exceptional man, long after he'd forgotten Mesa Vista, Moritomo Province.

He looked at the sky. Forget Mesa Vista? He doubted that would happen soon, if ever.

Carla fetched him soup and steak, standing over him with hands on hips, forcing him to clean up his plate and drink the lousy milk.

Then she fussed around him, replacing the dressing on his shoulder, checking the rapidly improving leg. He indicated that he meant to take a ride around town and she scolded him for his stupidity. He did not blame her, but knew he would do exactly as he said. He might have won one hand in this game, but that didn't mean it was over. With men of the Toro and Santo calibre involved, you could never claim victory until the last bullet was fired.

He smiled when she called him *estupído*. He told her he thought she was getting fat. She countered with the hope he might get gangrene in his leg, and he insisted that even that would be preferable to listening to her carp all day.

They both broke into laughter and Stocker glanced across at Don Luis, who was watching them closely with a distant expression in his eyes, as if he were thinking of another girl who had also laughed and been young.

Stocker eventually ordered Carla back inside for his Stetson. When she returned he limped across to where his horse was tied up. He swung up a little stiffly and rode off across the square.

When he quit the square he walked the sorrel through a maze of side streets and alleys. He knew he'd been weakened by blood loss and the afternoon sun soon brought the sweat coursing down his face.

The town was unnaturally quiet,

seemingly completely subdued by Santo's perceived defeat at his hands. Many of the faces he encountered were no longer filled with hate, while some even showed a grudging respect.

His prime reason for this patrol was to allow them to see him and know he was anything but incapacitated. That he was, in truth, very plainly physically capable should anybody want to test him out. They could not see the bullet furrow in his shoulder or the hole in his leg, and he hoped they didn't notice that he swayed a little in his saddle.

He rode for an hour before returning to the plaza where he swung down in front of the law office. He located Kwell and Fulton in the desk room with Trask, one of the guards. Ignoring the sheriff, whom he intended to have fired without pension directly after the execution, he talked briefly to Kwell before making his way down the corridor for the cells.

He was greeted with a storm of vilification from the prisoner, but did not respond, which seemed to enrage Toro all the more.

It was plain that Toro had altered greatly over the past twenty-four hours. Some of his arrogance appeared to be missing, the former sneering insolence now replaced by outright rage. The man even appeared thinner, with a gauntness hollowing boyish cheeks. The total failure of Santo's attempt to change his situation would have been devastating.

'You can start counting the hours before you pay for all the good people you've put in the ground now, Toro,' Stocker responded, turning to go. The cell doors clattered as the outlaw shook them violently, screaming profanities after him.

Stocker unhitched the big horse and led him towards Don Luis's house. He would have ridden the short distance but wasn't sure he had the strength to mount right now. He'd dispatched Carla to the mail office earlier with his report to Ballentine, so there was nothing more to be done at the moment.

He tied up the horse and went heavy-footed up the path.

He found Carla waiting at the big double doors. Taking one glance at his grey features and sweat-soaked shirt, she took him by the arm and hustled him through to the high-walled room in back where he slept. After ordering him to undress, she hurried off to fetch hot water and bandages. Obediently he did as ordered, too weak even to argue, knowing he must rest or pack up. The boots gave him the most difficulty, but he persevered grimly. He was damned if any females were going to undress him. Eventually he succeeded in getting them off, shucked off his clothes and fell heavily upon the bed.

Carla returned with the Trinidads' ancient cook; both women were laden with kettles, dishes and yards of bandaging. They cleansed and dressed the wounds, clucking at the hole in his lower leg. They bathed him and made him comfortable. The cook disappeared to prepare some food for him while

Carla seated herself at his bedside and cooled his forehead with a damp cloth. He wanted to order her to quit but it felt too good. So he just let her get on with it; it seemed a lot easier that way.

She disappeared at length to fetch the food. When she returned a bare minute later Stocker was in a deep sleep, the counterpane over his chest rising and falling to the even rhythm of his breathing.

Carla placed the bowl on the table and stood beside the bed for a long time, looking down at him. She bent low, her lips brushing his.

'Sleep well, *mi caro*,' she whispered.

★ ★ ★

Toro paced to and fro in his cell, five steps forward, five steps back. The sound of his high-heeled Mexican boots echoed in the stillness. The sun had gone, the cell was gradually darkening about him.

Today had been the worst day.

Standing upon his bunk he had witnessed the big gun battle at the cantina but had refused to believe the evidence of his own eyes. At first.

But at last he was coming to accept most of it and the bloody reality of it all rested heavily on his mind. If there was a single bright side it was the fact that Santo had blasted his way out of this stinking town, maybe with one or two of the others with him.

And where the hell was his gang?

For the harsh reality remained that his band from the south had not appeared; Santo had failed here, and in the end Stocker was the only one to walk away with head held high.

So hard to take!

Every minute he had languished in prison he'd been confident that he would find himself able to break out at any time with the help of his brave *bandidos*, maybe shoot up a couple of lawdogs, then hightail it back to the safety of Santo's village and plan the revenge attack at leisure.

It was mortally hard to adjust to this new uncertain position he found himself in.

He'd had but one visitor that day and that galled him most.

Several days previously the lawdogs had found themselves forced to send in those wanting to see him two at a time to enable them all to get to pay their respects. The defection of the towners seemed the most bitter blow of all. They had abandoned him and turned yellow-dog in the face of Stocker's gun law, leaving him to sweat it out alone, and maybe hang after all.

As he prowled his barred cage now, Toro's fiercest hatred was not for Stocker or the lawdogs . . . but for the people of Mesa Vista who'd deserted him in his most desperate hour. A hundred visitors his first week behind bars, now one or two a day, if he was lucky.

And after all he had done for them!

Yellow-dog Judas bastards!

His big plan for Mesa Vista had been originally conceived as both a territorial claim and a warning to the government. Suddenly the enemy had become the town — and it would feel his vengeance the moment he was free.

Free?

He licked dry lips as he seized the unyielding bars. 'I'll make them all pay!' he raged. 'Just as soon as I am free!'

He sounded confident, but was he? When Santo had come to town his hopes had been sky high. Now what did he have left? Cherry, he brooded, just Cherry. There was no doubting that that redheaded gringo was greased lightning with the cutters and as mean as Satan's mother-in-law. But he had to be honest and admit he had never trusted that sonofa. Then again, he also knew Cherry genuinely wanted to see him out of this jailhouse in order that he, Toro, might get to put Stocker in the ground to even old unsettled scores between those gringo gunslingers.

He nodded his curly head, feeling more confident now, making himself feel that way.

The bust-out would still happen, and between them he and his band would surely get to put Stocker in the ground where he belonged.

But only after he had dealt with this turncoat yellow town, he vowed. His head bobbed. That was how it would be. Town first, Stocker second.

Toro smirked in the half-dark, focusing on Stocker now. He wasn't so much, he had to believe. He'd been told the gunslinger had gone loco when Maria had been killed, while Toro, who had been her true love, had remained unmoved.

Of course he'd ranted and threatened on hearing that news, but that had been stage-managed in the hope that it might lead to the town rising up and stringing the gunfighter from the new gibbet.

Underneath all the uproar and hysteria, the girl's death had left him unaffected. Sure, she had been beautiful, and loco about him in a highly satisfying way. But to him any female's value was both limited and specific.

Maria had wished to marry him — not the other way round. For he could get any female he wanted without marrying them.

He blinked slowly, the thought of women leading on to thoughts of freedom and open spaces.

He slammed his boot viciously into the cell door.

'Hey, you gringo *cochinos*! Bring me the light. You think that Toro sees in the dark like a stinking bat?'

★   ★   ★

Cherry didn't finally make up his mind to bust Toro out until Tite Fulton reeled into the small grubby cantina hard by the mail office.

It was just after ten when the sheriff arrived and for the past hour Cherry had been lounging in the near-deserted *posada*, drinking sotol and chafing over events of the past twenty-four hours.

The man of the gun had witnessed the big shoot-out from a corner nearby, had seen Stocker tie into those *bandidos* and chop them down like so many sheep to the slaughter.

At the time he had congratulated himself for turning down Santo's invitation to join the band in the execution of the governor's guntipper.

For after witnessing Stocker in action against weighty odds he'd realized he would never now have the guts to face the man on level terms, and so had toyed with the notion of pushing on north and kicking the stinking mud of Mesa Vista off his fancy boots. Yet he had stayed. For there was still Toro. You could wager real money that Johnny Toro would never allow Stocker to ride off into the sunset should he get free.

Stocker had come here to make sure Toro hanged — Toro could never forgive or forget that.

Cherry nodded. Sure, he could rely on Toro to put Stocker in the ground. But how to get him free? He half-grinned in the cool gloom. Hell! That couldn't prove too hard with the sheriff on the booze again and Stocker limping around like some gouty old uncle!

Or so he had been, he reminded himself. Better make sure first. Maybe old 'have another' Fulton might unwittingly give him some ideas on how it might best be done?

He went to the bar.

'Evenin', Sheriff.' He smiled. 'Join me in a drink?'

'Why, er . . . sure, sure, young fella. Cherries, ain't it?'

'Cherry. One Cherry.' He signalled the barkeep. 'A double for my pard the sheriff, Guarta.'

Under the gunman's skilful probing and the tongue-loosening spirits, Fulton proceeded to inform his new pard that Kwell and Trask were at present guarding the jail. Cherry deftly shifted the topic to Stocker, and the lawman turned querulous.

'That hardnose? Would you believe he's going to see I lose my job and this badge after the hanging — gonna see me kicked out of the service for . . . for incontinence . . . no, incompetence and — '

'Terrible,' Cherry said sympathetically, topping up the peace officer's glass. He leaned confidentially closer to the man, peering around over his shoulder first, then said, 'Ain't you scared he might march right in here and catch you boozing again? He could get pretty mad, you know. That Stocker is a mean one.'

Fulton winked at him slyly.

'He won't come here or anyplace else tonight . . . no sir, not tonight.' He paused and drew the other in close. 'Tell me, can you keep a secret, Cherries?' The gunman nodded and Fulton whispered conspiratorily, 'Truth is, Stocker's snoring like a hog right now. He's pretty shaky and doped up for that leg wound he's toting. Trask told me he's off duty but warned me the word ain't to get around.'

He waved an admonitory finger in Cherry's face.

'You won't breathe it to a soul, will

you, Cherries? I only told you because you're a friend.'

'That's nothing but the simple truth, Sheriff,' Cherry assured, keeping his elation well-hidden. 'Bottoms up and we'll have us another.'

He would never get another opportunity like this, Cherry mused, studying his reflection in the back-bar mirror. Fulton drunk and Stocker on his back? It was like an open invitation.

Feeding Fulton another couple of double sotols to keep him soused and harmless, he bade him a cheery farewell and soon quit the cantina.

On the plankwalk he stood for a minute looking out over the square and thinking fast and clear. The plaza was quieter than he had seen it, the locals obviously intent upon keeping off the streets as Toro's execution date rushed closer by the moment.

It would doubtless remain quiet in Mesa Vista until after the hanging had taken place.

If . . .

Destiny hung in the balance for Cherry, for Mesa Vista and for Johnny Toro as the gunslinger rolled and lighted a smoke and stood leaning against an upright, inhaling deeply.

Stocker!

It was time to make a big decision about that gunslick and in so doing, analyse his own secret fears and weaknesses.

Stocker scared him.

There, he'd admitted it at last. Cherry had always regarded himself as one of the best, had cut down some top shooters in his time, made a big name and a lot of money with the Colts.

For a time here he'd conned himself that the involvement of Stocker in a big and risky job he'd agreed to take on didn't really bother him.

But now, having had time to witness him in action and understand what made him tick, he was worried and fretful.

Bust Toro out and make himself a big piece of money? Sure. It had sounded fine. Then came Stocker. He could envision himself carrying out the jailbreak successfully, and Toro coming up with the big *dinero*.

It was what might follow that kept him awake at night. For Stocker would come after him and who could say the bastard would ever quit? What man in his right mind would want that hard-nosed son of a bitch camped on his trail for — who could say how long?

But now that he had faced his demons Cherry was feeling clear-headed again. Sure, he would spring Toro. Toro planned to kill Stocker when he was free — after he'd carried out his big plan for this town which was calculated to teach the governor and the whole stinking country not to mess with Johnny Toro again.

The only change in plans now would be that they would take Stocker first — then Toro could stampede all the cattle in the Territory all over the Territory, if that was going to make him feel big and important.

Simple.

He headed directly for the law office.

Both Kwell and Trask started nervously and lifted their guns when he suddenly appeared to climb the steps on to the jailhouse's shadowed front porch, replacing them when he grinned and they recognized him.

Jumpy, he thought. And they had plenty of reason to feel that way.

'Howdy, Cherry.' The deputy grinned. 'This here is Trask, Territorial guard.'

The gunman nodded in acknowledgement, then turned back to Kwell, his expression sober. 'I just seen the sheriff,' he told him.

Kwell frowned and squinted. 'So? Anything wrong?'

'Plenty,' Cherry replied gravely. 'You know Joe's saloon, I guess?' The place was the drinking-hole furthest from jailhouse and square. The other nodded and he went on: 'Well, the sheriff is down there, drunk as a loon and threatening to arrest everyone in sight. Crazy!'

'Damn it to hell!' Kwell exploded.

'He was likkered up some when he left here, must've really tied into the stuff after.' He looked indecisively from one man to the other. 'I feel I ought to go fetch him. But he told me not to leave the office tonight. Stocker said there's got to be at least two of us keeping watch here at any given time . . . what with all these rumours about a possible bust-out, and all.'

'Well, I dunno about that,' Cherry pondered. 'Trouble is, he's liable to get his head busted or even a knife in the ribs down in that hell-hole.' He paused. Both Trask and Kwell looked concerned. 'Listen, what say I stay here with Trask and you go fetch the sheriff, Kwell. That way there'll be still two of us here all the time.'

Kwell deliberated a long moment before coming to a decision.

'Hell,' he said at last. 'Why not? It's quiet as a tomb in town right now and I'm not seriously expecting any trouble over Toro to blow up. Looks like Stocker really put the lid on the town last night, good and proper.' He picked up his hat. 'All right, I'll take you up on your offer, Cherry, and get back just as quick as I can.'

He strode off importantly, telling himself as he had been doing all week that he was Mesa Vista's only reliable peace officer at the moment. The deputy held high hopes of filling Fulton's boots after the sheriff was fired for dereliction of duty and that day could not come fast enough.

Cherry and Trask exchanged glances and the gunfighter casually led the way inside.

'Sure gets to worry a man when a sheriff forgets his duty,' Cherry said soberly. He fished the makings from his shirt-pocket and proffered them. 'Smoke?'

'Don't mind if I do,' replied Trask, a pale-faced man with a thickening waistline. 'Helps pass the time.'

Cherry appeared to fumble and his tobacco pouch dropped at the man's feet. He made an awkward move to retrieve it.

'I'll get it,' said Trask, who was closer.

The man bent down, and with the speed of a striking snake Cherry whipped out a gun and brought it thudding down upon the lowered head. Trask grunted, falling to his knees, and the barrel thudded home a second time. Trask sprawled against the desk, out to the world with blood seeping into his hair.

Cherry closed the door giving on to the plaza and shuttered the windows. Without glancing at the unconscious guard he took the keys down from the wall and, whistling soundlessly to himself, went through the archway leading to the cells.

9

Killer on the Loose

Johnny Toro was free.

He reined in atop a cottonwood slope several miles from the town, fished a long cigarillo from his shirt-pocket and set it alight. It was mid-morning with the sun brassy and hot on the slope, a jaybird calling from the hills behind.

The rider paid no attention to his surroundings. Below him and to the east a sizeable herd of longhorns was making its slow way along the trail route, with 200 burning miles still between them and the railhead at Diamondback Plain. Both the lowing of the cattle and the occasional yell of a cowboy drifted up to him as a great pall of reddish-brown dust sluggishly climbed into the sky to the rear.

Leaning forward on the pommel of

the stolen saddle, Toro smoked and studied the herd with bright and calculating eyes. He was bare-headed, his face still gaunt and pale from his imprisonment. The fancy white shirt was unbuttoned to the waist, tightfitting *charro* pants tucked into boot-tops. Buckled around slim hips hung two walnut-butted Colt .45s — Cherry's guns, which that fast-handed gun-tipper would not be needing any longer.

They'd been two miles clear of the town following the breakout when Cherry had suddenly halted and looked back.

'Nothing.' He grinned. 'Not a sign of pursuit. They don't even know you're gone yet, *amigo*. I gotta say this was one of my neatest jobs.'

'Very neat.'

'So, I've got my money, you're free as a jaybird. So I guess this is *adios*, Johnny.'

'Not quite.'

'Huh?' Cherry studied him closely. 'What do you mean . . . not quite?'

Toro smiled as he gestured languidly south-east. 'I still need you, *amigo* . . . you and that fast gun of yours. You see, when that lousy stinking town just gave up on me and left me to hang, I decided they would pay.'

'Pay? How do you mean . . . pay?'

Toro gestured lazily.

'Their lousy town will go tonight, *amigo*. Hey! You look surprised, but you can believe Toro. They will pay for deserting him in his peril, and the destruction of Mesa Vista will show the governor that they do not rule the south-east Territory any longer. That Toro is the power and shall remain so evermore . . . '

Cherry was a hard man to surprise. He was surprised now, and suddenly just a little wary.

'And just how do you plan to wipe out a whole town?' he asked sceptically.

'The big stampede. And all of the cows and my brave *compañeros* are waiting for us to join them right now.' He waved his arm in a graceful gesture to the south-east. 'Just an hour from here. Then the stampede will take but half that time to reach the town.'

Toro paused to smile winningly.

'It is all planned and all shall be well. But in the event of trouble it will be far better for me to have the great gunfighter Cherry by my side So, *amigo*, we go?'

'Go?' Cherry's face was cold. 'You can go straight to hell! We made a deal, Toro. I cracked you free, you paid me a thousand. OK, we've both kept our part of the deal, and that's it.'

Toro studied the American for a long moment in blank silence. Then he threw his head back and laughed.

'Ah, *amigo*, I see I make the big mistake when I think I can make you risk your neck again. You cannot blame a man for trying, no?'

He pushed his horse closer and reached out to clap the scowling gunfighter's slender back. 'No?'

'Mebbe not,' Cherry muttered, still frowning but relaxing some.

'Well said. Come. We ride to the top of the hill and then make our farewell like men of honour with the job well and bravely done behind them.'

They started up the gentle slope in the moonlight side by side with Toro laughing and joking and Cherry soon responding to his high spirits.

As they approached the crest Toro slowed his horse to make his way around a deadfall, the other continuing on directly upwards.

Faster than the blink of an eye Toro whipped out his .45 and three soft-nosed bullets thudded into Cherry's back.

Toro delayed only long enough to dismount and relieve the gunman of his valuables and beautiful sixguns, then he sprang into the saddle again with the lightness of an acrobat.

'Let us push on, *amigo*,' he told his horse, slapping the reins.

He rode leisurely into the hills, hipping around several times to confirm that the shots had not drawn attention.

He smiled at the spectacle of the sleeping herd when he topped out the hill that eventually brought them into sight, but it was anything but a good smile.

He rode right on by.

Somehow he had managed to defeat both Mesa Vista and the hangman with both dignity and reputation intact, but only he knew about the dark nights of the soul he had endured, the fear and humiliation. A man like Johnny Toro did not forget such things, could not. The imminent execution of his murderous plan to burn the name of Johnny Toro into the American consciousness filled his head excitingly as the swift horse-miles slipped away behind.

His spirits soared as he travelled on. Vengeance against Stocker for accepting money to guarantee his hanging; vengeance against Mesa Vista and its people, so many of whom had deserted and even reviled him once the enemy locked him in a cage.

For years now, ever since gunning

down three Territorial officers on the square of Mesa Vista, he'd been an idol and figurehead to the poor, the down-trodden and all those ancestral haters of the gringo.

That adulation had been like a powerful drug to a man of his towering vanity. For a long time he had been unable to pay for food or drink in Mesa Vista, his merest whim carrying the authority of a command with men and women vying with one another for the honour of serving him.

His fall had come overnight and had been devastating. In a vengeance attack upon an outlaw rival one night, he'd attacked the man's headquarters and riddled the place with bullets. An innocent bystander, two women and two children were found in the smouldering remains of the adobe next day.

On his run-out the horse had fallen and broken its foreleg and the killer was knocked unconscious, only to awaken behind bars.

Within a week Maria Trinidad had become his only regular visitor. He had been exploiting the girl's mad infatuation with him by passing messages through her to his henchmen, until she lost her life.

He had not wasted one tear on her, his fury at Stocker being nothing more than a sham. But in losing her he was left with the bare skeleton of his former twenty-strong band of hellers. Only the fanatics still retained a kind of tattered loyalty. But the man in the Mesa Vista street had turned his back on him, and that man would now reap the whirlwind of his wrath.

The betrayers, the lawdogs and particularly both Ballentine's hangman and the gunfighter, Stocker.

He licked his lips and began to sing. He was alone now but not for long. The remote hills hid his hard-core of henchmen. Not scurvy bootlickers like those scum who'd deserted him in the town but men of the gun and gringo-haters who were waiting eagerly

204

to ride with him again.

The moon hung directly overhead as he eased the horse along a steep little arroyo, then sent it onwards towards a lone cottonwood resembling a grounded green cloud atop a swaleback ridge.

He topped out the ridge, and beyond the low hummock of the hill, a plume of blue woodsmoke drifted straight up into the night sky.

Hoofs clattered sharply upon bare stone.

He'd selected the hard ground ever since quitting the ridges overlooking the trail route. He was not seriously anticipating pursuit. But should anyone, namely Stocker, be hunting him by this time, then he would need to be the Territory's finest sign reader to track him across this stretch of flinty country by night.

He scowled thoughtfully as the shadow of a hunting hawk flicked across the trail before him.

On second thoughts . . . maybe he should have left a trail? Allow Stocker to track him down, then wait in ambush and blow his gringo head off?

No. He must not overreach himself. First things first. The town first. Scholars would surely write of his deeds in the history books after he'd finished with that stinking haven for turncoats and gringo-lovers. And only after that was done would come the triumphant passion of the showdown with Stocker.

In the depression which came into view ahead stood half a dozen mud *jacals* with a backdrop of gnarled old cottonwoods and a tiny mountain stream running by. There was sand under the rider now, fine white banks of it sloping down to the stream with wild lilacs showing amongst the grass patches.

A woman crouched at the bank of the stream, washing clothing. A lone salt cedar threw moonshade over her face and bare arms. She did not hear his approach. A man was squatting before a hut with his back to him and three scraggy *burros* stood hipshot with heads hanging in a rude corral.

Once this had been a village of

hunters and prospectors. The Indians had massacred the entire town which had lain empty and ghost-ridden for twenty years until stumbled upon in its remoteness by a band of killers on the run from the law in Mexico.

It had proved the perfect hideaway for Toro's henchmen ever since.

'*Hola!*' he bawled.

The woman leapt to her feet in alarm. From the nearest *jacal* a man came running carrying a rifle in one hand and stuffing his shirt into his pants with the other. He propped on sighting the horseman. Men and women emerged from the other huts and someone cried out, 'It is Toro! He has risen from the grave!'

The rider whipped off his hat and waved it like a conquering hero as he pushed his mount across the stream and reined in amongst them.

One man grabbed the horse's head-stall, another patted the rider's knee as though to assure himself that it wasn't a vision but the genuine article — the one they often called, '*patron*'.

Toro removed his hat and sat his saddle, savouring the moment. The moonlight gleamed upon his smooth unlined face, teeth flashing in a handsome smile. At least he commanded total respect out here, he mused. They had not forgotten him or been willing simply to sit back and do nothing while the days, hours and minutes tick-tocked his young life away as had happened at Mesa Vista.

They might well be scum. But they were loyal and faithful scum. And their reward would be great. For Mesa Vista had long been a symbol of government oppression for the *Americanos* in this harsh south-east corner of the Territory. With that place destroyed he confidently expected Ballentine to find himself forced to wash his hands of the entire region, which would leave it free to slip into the hands of whoever had the strength to control it.

Himself.

He winked at a young girl, maybe

fifteen or sixteen. She was slender and olive-skinned, her body already curving into lush ripeness. She winked back boldly and fingered her blouse a little lower. Her father standing nearby saw the interchange and beamed proudly.

'How did you escape the prison, Johnny?' someone yelled.

'Why, I just walked out, *amigo*,' he replied. He snapped his fingers. 'Just like that.'

A chorus of admiring cries, and then, 'We hear so many evil rumors of what is happening in the town . . . we were sure you would perish.'

'But now Toro is back,' an old man cried excitedly, 'and he will surely keep his promise to take our ancient lands back from that evil gringo governor!'

'And so I shall, Disederio,' he assured. 'But we have something to do first . . . is that not so, my great *amigo*?'

Yaqui Santo stepped forward and smiled broadly. He had made it safely back to the hideaway following the saloon shoot-out, and Carlos and the delayed band from the south had shown up just few a hours later. Santo had feared it might be all over for Toro. He came to him now and they hugged each other and hefted bottles and some of the women began humming ancient war songs of old Mexico.

Santo stepped back and tugged his forelock in a gesture of fealty to his leader.

'Do we now strike, Johnny?'

'We strike, *compañero*, we surely do strike.'

'To wipe out our enemies and reclaim the lands of our forefathers?' A bearded giant recited like a litany the words that had been drummed into his great curly head, using the words of Toro himself.

'Why else would I be here?' Toro replied, looking every inch the stalwart leader of men as he flung an arm northwards.

'Get the men mounted and we are on our way to Oxtail ranch, Pancho!'

'Bravo Toro!' the big man bawled. The chant was taken up and was still to be heard long after the armed riders went storming off into the night a short time later.

★ ★ ★

The Oxtail nighthawks guarding the big herd didn't stand a chance. They had been under close watch for two weeks, and the riders who came by night found them only too easy to stalk and deal with.

Then the gates of the holding acres were opened and 500 half-asleep long-horns were pouring out on to the free range and being pointed north-west.

Hooting and hollering and cracking their long bulltail whips, the Mexicans quickly had the herd fully awake and rumbling swiftly across the open plains. It was no longer a running mob but a roaring stampede by the time the first dim lights showed in the vastness of the night far ahead.

The face of Toro was something to see.

10

Gallows Walk

A ragged *campesino* ran into the *placita* screaming. 'Stampede . . . stampede!' his skinny arms flailing above his head and his eyes bulging in total terror.

There had already been much noise and excitement upon the streets of Mesa Vista that night. For had not the great Toro escaped and galloped away, leaving no trace behind? Seemingly gone also was all fear of the gringo pistoleer, Stocker . . . the capricious loyalty of the town switching instantly to the apparent victor. Guitars, accordions, fiddles and pianos, all were in full cry tonight, adding boisterously to the gaiety at Armijo's, the Blue Duck, Fat Manuel's and every squalid tequila bar in town.

The fears, uncertainties and forebodings that had tainted their sorry lives for so long seemed no more and men and women laughed and danced and drank the wine. And barely anyone heard the cry, 'Who is that drunken fool screaming out there on the *placita*?'

A lone longhorn, red-eyed and furious, clattered noisily into the Plaza of Heroes. A noisy bunch of revellers, swinging arm in arm between Armijo's and the Blue Duck stopped abruptly in mid-song at sight of the slobbering beast lurching past the gallows.

'*Nombre de Dios!*' one gasped as they grew aware of the ominous trembling beneath their feet followed by a mounting roaring and bellowing which was pierced suddenly by the terrible scream of a man in agony.

Moments later the massed leaders of the stampede spewed into the square.

The crazed cattle slowed in the sudden glare of the lights, with eyes rolling and tails twitching, until the enormous press from behind forced them on. A communal cry of terror rose, bringing figures boiling out of the cantinas and hovels to quake with instant terror and then attempt to outrun the onrushing red-and-white flood.

One man, encircled by the swirling nightmare in the centre of the square, emptied his sixgun into the mindless mass and was instantly swallowed beneath them. In an endless wave they came, score upon score of the meanest, wildest critters on the face of the plains, some boasting horn spans of over ten feet with needle-sharp points, some of which even now were glistening blood-red.

Riders burst in from the side streets, trying to turn them, triggering into the mob, but without cohesion or pattern. Some citizens went down quickly while others whirled to go, fleeing for dear life as the carnage threatened to engulf them all.

Boardwalks crumpled and splintered, porch uprights snapped with reports like rifle shots. Sun-dried timbers collapsed like papicr-mâché as thirty-feet-long galleries collapsed under the sheer weight and power of the unstoppable flood. Oil-lamps crashed down as dust rose thickening to choke the very air, blinding those attempting to escape. And now flames leapt upwards in bright crimson columns to lick their hungry tongues around tinder-dry timbers, consuming them in mere moments, hungrily rushing onwards to devour more and more.

The red glare of the fires leapt higher, mingling with the blinding dust, adding fiercely to the terror . . . driving the beeves to madness.

By now terrified citizens filled every street running off the square. Half-blinded cattle, crazed by fear and clamour, burst headlong through the doors into the cantinas, scattering the cowering crowds. Men and women clambered atop tables and bars, anywhere to escape bloodied horns and hammering hoofs.

Windows and mirrors exploded into shivering shards of dagger-pointed glass as some survivors continued triggering insanely into the herd, some to fall instantly, others to survive just a little longer.

Out on the plaza a group of riders, mostly *vaqueros* from the ranches, galloped their mounts alongside the herd. They were attempting to turn the living flood into two of the wider streets which led down to the river, but at the last moment the leading bunch doubled back blindly, crashing head-long into the riders, horns ripping into horseflesh until one by one the gallant riders went down.

The rumble of hoofs and screams of terror were now joined by the even greater roar of the flames as fire after fire erupted in the wake of the stampede.

And the dust-choked sky boiled red and sinister over a town facing death.

★　★　★

The sheriff was at the bar of the Blue Duck close by the law office when he heard the sudden uproar on the square.

He set his glass upon the bar and felt the vibrations coming up through the floorboards, wondering whether this was merely some new manifestation of his alcoholic stupor. A man ran screaming into the dingy room. 'Stampede! There's a herd rushing through the square and we're all gonna die!'

Fulton watched the bottles trembling on the shelves as hoofs drummed across the plankwalk directly outside. Then a great longhorn thundered blindly into the room itself, with a slatted door hanging from one horn.

The beast charged, smashing chairs and tables aside as men and women screamed and ran.

And then a small miracle occurred.

Almost as though he'd been preparing for this moment in the spotlight all his life, the sheriff of Mesa Vista calmly whipped out his .45 and, standing straight and tall, began blasting at the maverick bull at almost point-blank range. Blood, bone and horn splinters flew into the air but the animal seemed impervious to pain and injury until the very last moment when, almost upon the strangely heroic figure of the sheriff of Mesa Vista, its forelegs gave way as though scythed off, the big body struck the floor with a reverberating crash, rolled over, kicked once and died.

Fulton stared dumbly at the gun in his fist. Then another animal showed in what was left of the doorway. He whipped out a derringer and clipped the beast's snout with the first shot. It slithered on the bloodied floor, sighted a half-open door and went charging headlong back out into the insane night.

'All right, you people!' the sheriff shouted, leaping on to the bar to snatch down the saloonkeeper's Greener. 'Calm down and arm yourselves. We're going to turn this mob and we're going to do it now! Every man Jack of us.'

They stared. Nobody had taken one lick of notice of their sheriff since he started seriously on the bottle.

The Greener roared and a side door splintered.

'Now, not tomorrow week — you sons of bitches!'

They were terrified of what was happening outside. They were even more afraid of a drunken lawman with a big rifle who in that electrifying moment looked far more dangerous and determined than any 1,000-pound steer.

Every man had a weapon of some description by the time the sheriff led them to what had been the front door.

'We're going to turn the point of the stampede and steer them out along Tin God Street to the river flats,' he announced. 'I'll put a bullet in any man shows yellow!'

So saying, the town's unlikeliest hero led them out into the madness of the night.

*   *   *

Don Luis Trinidad sat at the window of his book-lined study, methodically emptying his beautiful if old-fashioned lever-action ball repeater into the beasts which had flattened the fence of his garden but had thus far failed to intrude any further.

A growing mound of carcasses out front, half-covering the walkway, testified to his accuracy and firepower. In the room in back of him his three manservants reloaded both his gun and those of O'Brien, the Territorial guard who was guarding the south side of the house.

'Courage, Minna, courage,' he murmured gently to the ancient cook who stood trembling and unmovable in her shock. The strong, calm voice soothed both the old woman and everybody else in the huge room, including O'Brien. Don Luis was not afraid.

* * *

In an alcove of her rooming-house, Donna Salla knelt before a tiny altar. Her lips moved silently, her eyes glued to a carved wooden cross. On either side of the cross stood a lighted candle which fluttered wildly as the whole building rocked and shook from the passing of the herd close by.

Carla stood in the doorway of her room, watching open-mouthed as the living red sea flowed by below. She started at a gurgling scream, averted her face sharply as a red-and-white steer appeared with the writhing figure of a man impaled upon one horn.

'Stocker,' she sobbed aloud, 'come quickly . . . *rapidamente. Dios mio*, make him come quickly . . . make him safe!'

Stocker overtook the tail of the herd before it reached the centre of town. He lashed the sorrel onwards until he drew slowly ahead of the lead animals at the head of the last bunch.

'Yeeehahhh!' he roared, triggering his sixgun almost in their ears.

The cattle were drooping from their mad run and as yet had not been inflamed by the fires and hysteria up ahead. They held their course for a hundred yards before Stocker clipped the shoulder of the lead bull with a bullet, causing it to swerve abruptly into the mouth of the first street. The rest followed — as Stocker had intended they should. Instantly the whole mob was now flowing southward and away from the smoke- and dust-shrouded town.

'So far so good!'

Stocker was ready to applaud every advantage he might seize upon at this stage. He knew what lay ahead, had blocked out his plan for dealing with it — if and when he survived that far. The rest lay in the lap of the gods.

* * *

The sea of red backs was being swallowed up by the dark plains safely away from the town by the time Stocker led his men back into the south-east sector of what had once been a tolerably solid sector of town.

He rode grimly past crumbling *jacals*,

blazing barns and stalls . . . glimpsed mad-eyed citizens running aimlessly . . . the bodies of dead and dying beeves.

It was bad. Yet, so he already sensed, not nearly as bad as it might have been.

He hauled his lathered mount to a halt on gaining the plaza. A nightmare scene greeted him on the southern side with half the structures afire or already fallen. Even as he watched, a flood of fire was washing away across a sweep of sun-dried grassland to the south-east, leaving behind errant spot-fires which, despite their lack of volume were nonetheless attacking the padre's house, licking hungrily up the walls. Those who'd taken refuge in the solid stone church immediately came pouring out, adding to the chaos.

He signalled to two drovers, who instantly spurred across to the church, sprang down and set about beating out the flames with blankets supplied swiftly by the plump padre.

Stocker thanked his stars he'd

encountered these riders making back for home along the border. They were tough, trail-hardened men who seemed to know instinctively what he wanted, what needed to be done. Practically every citizen he'd sighted here in town appeared to be on the edge of hysteria — and who could blame them? But the plainsmen had arrived here clear-eyed and capable, and he knew exactly how to make best use of them.

He'd done his planning on the ride in. He'd encountered more damage than he'd hoped for but not nearly as much as he might have feared. His overview told him the stampede had stormed across the south-west corner of the plaza but had then veered away sharply down Strabo Street, eventually reaching open country again.

Right now, he calculated the main mob would be lumbering away through the southern slums, and that set his brain clicking like a telegraph key. Envisioning that sector, he saw Titus Street in his mind's eye — broad and angling south — towards the river flats.

He sleeved his mouth, calculating all that could go amiss with his plan. Then he reminded himself it was the only plan he had, that time was running out for the town, that, right or wrong, he must act. Now!

He gathered the horsemen about him with a gesture, told them what he planned to do, ordered a hairy-faced drover to shut up when he suggested it was impossible.

Then they kicked their prads into a gallop and headed for the turmoil of the southern sector of the reeling town.

It was worse than he'd feared when they reached the squalid southside slums, but they didn't hesitate. With Colts roaring and whips cracking, the riders hazed the milling herd together through some ten hair-raising minutes until at last they had them trotting rather than bolting in the general direction of smoke-shrouded Titus Street.

Whenever a beast attempted to break

away from the mob Stocker gunned it down. They must be kept tight otherwise they'd fragment all over what was left of the town and Mesa Vista would be finished.

The mouth of Titus Street yawned ahead. At a signal from Stocker the riders began hazing the beeves along faster, blasting gunshots in back of them. Soon they had them trotting, eventually running. Stocker kicked ahead and showed them the way, heeling his prad into Titus. A bull tossed its scimitar horns and made to break away but a bullet from behind brought the animal crashing down.

Now Stocker was in the street and the lead animals, slobbering, head-hanging and crazy-eyed by this time, were following him.

'Simple,' he grunted sardonically minutes later when at last he dropped out and allowed the herders to keep the stampede running in the right direction — towards the distant river. 'Or, more likely, just lucky.'

By the time he was nearing the square the vast bulk of the stampede would be spreading out harmlessly across the river flats to the south, and the fire-fighters could go to work in earnest in their wake.

Gaining the square and skilfully dodging small bunches of glassy-eyed beeves still running dazedly every which way, he glimpsed Don Luis's house still standing and virtually unscathed. He heeled the horse up to the crumbling fence and reined in.

'Don Luis!' he shouted. 'Carla there?'

The dim figure of Don Luis appeared in the front portico. He was pointing across the smoke-shrouded square. 'Armijo's . . . I think!'

Stocker sent his horse back into the dust and smoke, eventually to sight Armijo's, which had become a raging inferno with half its façade already fallen across the plankwalk into the plaza.

He narrowly avoided a fire-blinded steer which came out of nowhere in a rush, the sorrel barely avoiding slashing horns.

The single beast was followed by a sudden rush of some dozen or more, travelling just as fast and mindlessly as the blind critter. Stocker was forced to heel away for the safety of a tight little alley off to his right. He flattened his horse against a shallow dock in the wall in the half-dark as the cattle boiled towards his position. From out of the whirling darkness another horseman appeared, a big burning man with terrified eyes who attempted to wedge his way into the sanctuary with Stocker.

There was plainly barely sufficient room for one horsemen, much less two. He bawled at the man to keep going. The rider hesitated, then looked over his shoulder to see beeves rushing their way. He attempted to heel his mount into the confined space. Stocker leaned forward and smashed him almost out of his saddle with a brutal punch. The man jerked his horse around and hardly made it back to the mouth before a red-eyed beeve hit him like a freight train.

Stocker jerked out his revolver and pumped hot lead into the maddened beasts as they invaded his alley. In seconds there was a mound of bodies so deep that he was forced to dismount and, with great difficulty climb the horse back over the carcasses out into the square, where for the moment at least there was not a single stampeder left in sight.

He jumped astride and kicked on to Armijo's which was smoke-blackened but not burning. As he rode into the yard the first person he saw was Carla, kneeling and weeping by the tie rack alongside what the longhorns had left of Pedro Armijo.

He swung down and hauled the girl to her feet.

She gestured towards the shattered gateway. 'He ran out here to quieten his horse just as part of the mob broke away and came right through . . . '

Stocker was sympathetic but it didn't

show. With one motion he swept her up in his arms and boosted her into his saddle as a fresh drumming of hoof-beats sounded close by.

He was up behind her by the time a coal-black beeve came storming through the broken gate with others in sight behind. In one fluent motion he whipped out his Peacemaker and hammered three bullets into its skull. The beast cartwheeled at full gallop, barely missing the double-laden horse. Before those animals trailing their leader could make the yard, Stocker was kicking away and heading back across the deadly square for the safety of Don Luis's white house.

★ ★ ★

Mesa Vista lay stunned in the wake of the chaos.

In the grey hour before dawn, men, women and children emerged from wherever they had found sanctuary, silent and hollow-eyed, moving dazedly through some sectors which had been totally unaffected by the stampede, then halting wordlessly on confronting burnt-out buildings or the occasional bloodied corpse.

Solitary longhorns still wandered aimlessly through the streets and out upon the square. Eventually they would be driven out to the main herd which was now grazing placidly along the north bank of the river, crazed and fearsome no longer.

Considering the wholesale destruction that might have resulted had the path of the stampede not been diverted, and had the fires not been eventually confined mainly to the south-west quarter, the overall picture was positive and already some of the hardier and more practical citizens were setting about the business of cleaning up and restoration. As this progressed, Stocker's drovers were to be seen hazing the surviving beeves out on to the flats.

Around the plaza a dozen buildings had been destroyed, several were still smoking. Smoke-blackened patches on a further score of dwellings and business premises only showed how much more severe the outcome would have been had not so many pitched in and fought the fires despite the danger.

One prominent structure had remained standing with no visible signs of damage. Standing sturdily still upon its stone base above the reach of sweeping horns and separated by open space from blazing buildings during the long night, the gallows was framed against the sky.

* * *

The clatter of walking horses sounded loud in the stillness as from behind the husk of a burned-out barn a bunch of horsemen appeared. In silence they rode into the square and drew up before the gallows.

The man in the lead was Johnny Toro.

Ignoring the effect the bunch's

sudden appearance created, Toro lazily cocked one leg over his saddle horn and lighted up a cigarillo. His gaze drifted slowly around him, touching upon the hotel and the church with its fire-darkend cross. He gazed upon surviving structures and heaps of blackened ash and wreckage with equal indifference.

If he were disappointed that his brutal attempt to destroy Mesa Vista totally and leave it a pile of smoking rubble, he gave no sign. Indeed, taking his first leisurely look at what had been achieved, Johnny Toro ran fingers through his hair and smiled.

His men did not smile. Their faces were grave and fearful in the morning light, and more than one crossed himself at sight of the smoke-damage to the church. They had not fully realized what Toro's plan was when they had raided the big herd, and by the time they did it was too late. No man quit on Toro and lived. As a consequence, half of them had been killed or crippled in the mayhem, including Santo, the *segundo*.

But Toro himself was riding high, basking in his transition from rope bait to avenging hero — at least in his own eyes.

He was far too elated in his moment of 'triumph' to note the sullen stares, the angry whisperings behind upraised hands, the dangerous silence of the survivors as they emerged from hovels and ruins to stand and stare across the wide *placita*. His plan had been to destroy the entire town, but he would generously settle for one third.

He did not seem to know or care that it was only now that the word was sweeping through Mesa Vista that the stampede had been no tragic accident, as at first believed, but rather constituted a deliberate vengeance attack by Johnny Toro upon the town that had taken him captive and then had been quite happy simply to sit back and watch him swing.

In punishing those responsible for his suffering and humiliation, Toro had punished every citizen in the river town.

He didn't notice the hostility; even had he done so it could not have impinged upon his heady sense of triumph in those first dramatic moments.

He even feigned terror of the gibbet to his riders and they laughed because he laughed.

It seemed a long, taut time until he flipped his cigarillo butt away. He nodded and straightened his shoulders. His act of vengeance had been enough to satisfy him — up to a point. Never again would people dare turn against him, or desert him when he needed them. They would think of Mesa Vista and remember what had happened here.

And what was yet to happen.

His gaze now focused sharply upon the silent house of Don Luis.

'Stocker!' he called, his voice echoing in the stillness. 'Remember? This is the day of execution!'

There was no doubt in Toro's mind that Stocker had survived Mesa Vista's night of disaster. Even had every other man jack in this lousy town perished, he knew the gunfighter would have lived. He was that kind of man.

'Here I am, Toro!'

The voice had not come from the big white house but from another quarter. Toro turned lazily to see the familiar figure standing alone at the mouth of a side street. He was hatless and his hand hung close to his sixgun.

Toro's laugh was a hot knife in the stillness.

'What do you say, government man?' He waved a hand at the sky. 'An eye for an eye — a good day to die. That's what they say, or did I just make it up?'

'I knew you'd show, killer,' Stocker said. 'Knew you wouldn't be able to resist coming back to gloat and brag. Well, what you've really come back to do, is hang, just like the law says you must.'

Toro tossed his head back and laughed, sounding genuinely amused. Then sobered and said, 'You have to be loco, Stocker. Crazy. Who do you believe will back your play now I'm back, free, with guns and all my brave *amigos* at my side? You've always been a loner, but I'm telling you that you were never more alone than you are right here, right now. Like I reminded, this is execution day and we're going to have one. Yours!'

Toro hipped around in the saddle, still smiling. The smile froze as armed men, afoot, tough-faced Americans toting naked rifles, emerged silently from the ruins to form a menacing semicircle behind the outlaws.

Disbelievingly, Toro counted nine in all. Kwell, Trask and O'Brien he recognized, but the other six he'd never seen before.

He whirled ashen-faced to Stocker, who nodded.

'Territorial Guards, Toro!' he supplied. 'I sent Ballentine a wire when you busted out. These men happened to be just over in Candelaria with a gold shipment and the governor wired them to up stakes and get across here to help round you up. They only arrived two hours back but I've had them waiting ever since. Why? I knew this was your work just as I knew that no two-bit excuse for a badman like you would be able to resist showing up to admire his dirty handiwork. You just proved me right.'

Johnny Toro shook like a man with the ague, fury, disbelief and murderous rage all visible in his face. His eyes were like hot coals on Stocker, his face contorting into a mask of animal fury. Suddenly he sprang to ground, landed cat-light and took half a dozen fast steps towards his enemy.

'You'll go before I do!' he raged, slim hands hovering over twin guns. 'Go for your — '

'No, Stocker!'

It was Carla's cry coming from Trinidad's portico. Don Luis silenced her, then shouted, 'She is right, *compañeros*! Do not fight this scum. Let him hang!'

Stocker didn't reply. He was staring at Toro and when he spoke his voice shook with emotion.

'You reckon you've got grudges to settle with me, Toro? I'm the one with scores to settle. I've got Maria — so go for your irons and I'll see you die, *cabrón*!'

The killer hesitated as the gunfighter strode towards him, continuing to lash him with his tongue. Even the killer's own henchmen were astonished. None had seen Johnny Toro display uncertainty or hesitation in a crisis before. But he'd never faced a Stocker before. He'd heard that this man had never been beaten with the Colts, and was considered never likely to be. *A man faces Stocker and his blood turns to water!* was a saying he'd heard, and he was hearing it echoing inside his skull at that moment as the tall figure loomed dangerously close.

Turns to water? That was how his blood felt at that moment. *Not Toro! Never Toro!*

Both men slashed for gun handles in the same red moment. Toro was fast but

Stocker was faster. With gun crashes roaring deafeningly, Toro went staggering back staring down at his broken, bleeding gun arm.

Faster than light, he was grabbing for the piece left-handed when Stocker, moving like a canebrake panther, lunged forward. While Toro's clawing left hand was still empty Stocker lashed out with an iron fist that exploded against the killer's jaw while his gun was still but halfway out of its holster, smashing him to ground.

Stocker loomed above the dazed figure on the dark ground with the muzzle of his piece yawning in the faces of the killer's startled henchmen.

They had never seen Toro beaten before, had never seen sudden death in the eyes of an enemy as they did now in Stocker's.

'You'll all get your day in court — that's the best I can offer you if you get those hands up now,' he said in an iron voice. 'If you don't, I promise you I can kill you all before you'd get me.'

His words struck like daggers — straight to the heart. The senior hellion in the bunch rolled his eyes and slowly raised hands to shoulder height, and it was all over from that point. As men came forward to relieve them of their weapons, Stocker took his piece off full cock.

'Lock Toro up tight and — '

'You bastard!' Toro raged. 'All right, you have won, but kill me now, Stocker. One shot.'

Stocker allowed his gun to point to the ground.

'The governor didn't send me here to gunfight you, killer. He sent me here to make sure you hang. And hang you will . . . on the gallows decent men built for you.'

He turned away and walked towards Don Luis's, passing through clusters of wide-eyed citizens, some of whom spoke to him without drawing a response. For his eyes were on Carla as she rushed from the big double doors, down the flagged path, then threw

241

herself into his arms, sobbing with anxiety and laughing with relief at the one time.

He soothed her down then called to the house. 'Haley, you've a job to see to after all.'

Ethan Haley emerged from the house where he'd been lodged. The executioner was dressed with sombre dignity in black broadcloth. He nodded gravely and walked past Stocker and the girl with a solemn, measured tread. The Territorial executioner always believed a hangman should go about his work with dignity.

★ ★ ★

Johnny Toro was hanged at sunset in the square at Mesa Vista. Haley did his job professionally and Toro died bravely after confessing his sins to Padre Martinez. The survivors of the town witnessed it all, both from the high balconies of those places still standing and from the ashes of those which lay in charred ruins.

Governor Ballentine had warned that all Territorials must respect the law. They respected it now — in Mesa Vista.

★   ★   ★

His back to the onlookers upon the square, Stocker sat his big ugly sorrel and made his farewells to Don Luis and Carla.

'*Hasta la vista*, Don Luis,' he said simply. 'We'll meet again.'

'*Vaya con Dios*, Clay Stocker.'

He leaned from the saddle and the older man's grip was strong and true, for which Stocker would always feel grateful.

Then his eyes went to the girl and he felt an ache in his chest.

'*Hasta la vista*, Carla.'

'*Adios mio caro*.' He saw the tears.

The horse moved away slowly and he could feel her eyes on his back. Abruptly he reined in and the blunt question leapt into his mind, dominating, insistent: *What in hell are you doing?*

For a full minute he sat his saddle with his back to her, then suddenly he hipped around and looked at her with a strange intensity.

Barely seeming to breathe, the girl studied his face. Seconds passed in aching silence with neither moving, yet neither glancing away. And then he smiled . . . the first time she had ever seen a smile light his face and it seemed bright as the sun.

Stocker patted the horse's hindquarters and Carla came flying across to his side. Her eyes were enormous as she watched him draw his foot from the stirrup and reach down to seize her outstretched hand. She swung up behind him feather light, wrapping her arms tightly about his waist and her cheek pressed hard against his back.

Together they rode from Mesa Vista.

We do hope that you have enjoyed reading this large print book.

Did you know that all of our titles are available for purchase?

We publish a wide range of high quality large print books including:
Romances, Mysteries, Classics
General Fiction
Non Fiction and Westerns

Special interest titles available in large print are:
The Little Oxford Dictionary
Music Book, Song Book
Hymn Book, Service Book

Also available from us courtesy of Oxford University Press:
Young Readers' Dictionary
(large print edition)
Young Readers' Thesaurus
(large print edition)

For further information or a free brochure, please contact us at:
Ulverscroft Large Print Books Ltd.,
The Green, Bradgate Road, Anstey,
Leicester, LE7 7FU, England.
Tel: (00 44) **0116 236 4325**
Fax: (00 44) **0116 234 0205**

*Other titles in the
Linford Western Library:*

BOTH SIDES OF THE LAW

Hank J. Kirby

A full hand in draw poker changed Hardin's life — and almost ended it. First there was the shoot-out with the house gambler. Then suspicion of bank robbery, enforced recruitment into a posse, gunfights in the hills and pursuit by both sides of the law in strange country. He'd never had so much trouble! What should he do? Drift on, away from this hellhole, or stay and fight? There was no real choice — it was fight or die . . .

LIZARD WELLS

Caleb Rand

After losing his whole family to a bloodthirsty army patrol, Ben Brooke takes to the desolate Ozark snowline. Years later, he returns to the town called Lizard Wells, where the guilty soldiers have degenerated into guerrillas, bringing brutal disorder to the town. Also living there is the tough Erma Flagg — and more importantly, Moses, a young Cheyenne half-breed ... After a wild thunderstorm crushes the town, Ben, in desperate need of help, chooses to step single-handedly into a final reckoning.

MISFIT LIL FIGHTS BACK

Chap O'Keefe

Misfit Lil wouldn't allow the rustlers to run off some of her pa's improved Flying G beeves. She started a stampede that trampled them bloodily into the dust. But then two assassins gunned down horse rancher Sundown Sander's son Jimmie. And he had made no move to defend himself, despite Lil's stormy ride to bring him warning. Could devious madam Kitty Malone or gambling-hall owner Flash Sam Whittaker tell the truth about Jimmie's fatal resignation? Lil had to find out.

SHOOT-OUT AT BIG KING

Lee Lejeune

Billy Bandro arrives in Freshwater Creek in Wyoming to start a new life away from riding with the killer outlaw Wesley Toms. When Toms is captured, Billy is assigned to drive him to Laramie for trial, but Toms' gang bushwhack the coach, leave Billy for dead, and take Nancy Partridge and her Aunt Emily hostage. The gambler Slam Beardsley saves Billy, and they ride off in pursuit. But there are many surprises for them in the mountains . . .

ROLLING THUNDER

Owen G. Irons

The town, once a thriving community, was now rotten. Even Tyler Holt, who'd never been browbeaten, lay dead, lynched by a mob. It was all down to Tom Quinn, leader of the first settlers, to return Stratton to its former prosperity. Stratton Valley, with its lush grass, rightfully belonged to him, but what could he do? As he faced the might of Peebles and his cohorts who controlled Stratton, only his courage and gun skills could save the day . . .